A GRAVE GAMBIT

⩵ A FIONA MAHONEY MYSTERY ⩵

USA TODAY BESTSELLING AUTHOR

KERRIGAN BYRNE

OLIVERHEBERBOOKS

PUBLISHER'S NOTE: This is a work of fiction. Names, characters, places, and incidents either are the product of the author's imagination or are used fictitiously. Any resemblance to actual persons, living or dead, business establishments, events, or locales is entirely coincidental.

A Grave Gambit Copyright 2025 © Kerrigan Byrne

Cover by: Ravenborn Covers

Published by Oliver Heber Books

0 9 8 7 6 5 4 3 2 1

Chapter One

To cut the viscous slick of human blood from the gap between flagstones, it took three passes of carbolic and two of vinegar.

The first two were for the police—so the inspector could parade a "sanitized" scene to his curious gawkers—and again for the press.

The third was for myself—a fastidiousness born not of perfectionism, but of a kind of superstitious terror instilled in me by my father.

Leave too much of a murdered body in the place they died, and you tempted the dead to stay.

And so, I found myself in the same place I often did after midnight...couched on my haunches in the mist, a brush in one gloved hand and a flask of solution in the other, scrubbing the latest bit of butchery out of the world.

The two young constables, Hemmings and Sutherland, had retreated to smoke beneath the gas lamp at the corner of Lambeth, their forms blurred in the sulfurous two a.m. haze. Even at this remove, I could sense their nerves. It was in the uneasy glances they sent my way and in the increasing impatience in their gestures.

Footpads were often skittish in the aftermath of a violent death.

It was only a conception of murder until you saw the work up close.

Real, arterial blood never looked like the manufactured crimson seen on a stage. In the shadows of a gaslit London night, it was almost black, except where the rain's meager effort caused it to run down the walls of the shop.

Once I'd cleared off the steps, I turned to the lower brick of the pawn shop's threshold and paused, my forehead creasing in confusion. The blood spray was most telling, a tight, upwards fan, only a foot across. The perpetrator had stood square to the victim, close enough to smell her hair, and brought the blade up through her windpipe with the sort of economy that suggested skill.

Jack the Ripper had such skill.

Which was why I took every job I could when a woman was murdered with a knife...to see if his specter haunted her violent end.

I knew he was still alive and still in London.

He sent me letters.

This, however, was not his work, I noted with equal parts relief and disappointment.

It was a neat little scene, as these went. If the Metropolitan's new Murder Inquest Division had any sense, they'd call it a one-time crime of passion. A lover's quarrel? A debt settled?

An Irish matter?

That was what they all wanted: an Irish matter. Even in 1889, the English preferred to believe no Englishman would do something so animal as slice a woman's throat. They were always desperate to pin such acts on immigrants and the disenfranchised.

But that line of thinking only held if you ignored the actual evidence, which I did not.

My own little empire depended on the truth. The knowing of it and sometimes...the denying of it.

The dead were my business, and business was relentless. Which was good for my pocketbook, and terrible for my sleeping habits. I cringed as I tossed the bucket of soiled and soapy water at the wall I'd been scrubbing, watching with grim satisfaction as the last of the blood flowed in gruesome rivulets to the gutters.

"Done soon, Miss Mahoney?" called one of the constables, affecting casual interest as he drew on a reeking cigarette. "The coroner's cart is about to leave, and Old Boyle offered you a ride back toward home if you want it."

I did not want it. "Tell him not to wait. I'm no comfort, not even for the most desperate for company tonight," I said, letting just enough of my mother's brogue creep into the vowels to make him nervous. The driver, Christian Boyle, was Irish, but from the North...The constable wouldn't understand why I didn't get on with him.

He huffed and retreated, and I allowed myself a breath.

In the alley's close stillness, the copper tang of blood fought with my antiseptics, the combination oddly reminiscent of over-boiled cabbage. I imagined my grandmother squinting at me over a bubbling pot, muttering that I'd always had a taste for the unwholesome.

She wasn't wrong.

You didn't become London's foremost post-mortem sanitation specialist by accident, and you didn't keep the work unless you could compartmentalize your own disgust. I trained my mind to treat each job as a puzzle: How to remove a quart of blood from the grout of a secondhand shop floor before morning? How to neutralize the scent so the day clerks wouldn't vomit? How to arrange the body, once the police had had their look, so the kin could imagine her passing was more peaceful than it actually was?

You solved enough of these little riddles and the monsters of the city started to respect you.

Or, failing that, they at least learned to rely on you to clean up the blood they spilled.

I scraped another clot of tissue from the stone, dropped it into my waxed envelope, and glanced up. Nothing moved at street level, but above, in the dense blackness between windows, I felt eyes. Watching me work. Judging, perhaps, or just waiting for a chance to claim their own piece of the night.

I never grew used to that part, no matter how many times I played the ghoul.

I straightened, stretching the ache from my back. My hands shook, the fingers not from fatigue but from something colder—an old, private tremor that had plagued me since the last of the Ripper's jobs. Croft noticed it first, at the morgue, during one of his rare flashes of actual tenderness. "You'll wear yourself to bone," he'd said once, using the only diminutive I ever tolerated. "Who will plague me at murder scenes then?"

Inspector Grayson Croft, hero of the Marylebone slayings, newly promoted and already half-dead from the effort of pretending to care about the living. Our partnership (never more than strictly professional, I reminded myself) had dried up like a cadaver in the July heat.

I didn't blame him, exactly. I'd kept a secret from him for far too long...one I knew would cause him and his sister pain. My silence had cost me, and they paid in kind.

I'd heard from neither of them in months.

And then there was Aramis Night Horse. My first lover had vanished as suddenly as he'd appeared, leaving only the legend of how he'd finished Drumft and a handful of rumors darker than anything the papers dared print.

I tried not to miss him.

He was nothing if not a methodical murderer by trade, and while such a vocation actually supplements my own, we always understood our hearts would never align.

The only constant in my life at the moment was the Hammer—Jorah David Roth—whose letters continued to find me wherever I went. He paid well for the jobs I was unable to turn down.

My loyalty to Jorah wasn't bought. It was demanded. And if the Hammer ever questioned it, my life was forfeit.

There had been a time when I'd thought of myself as an honest woman, but in the Hammer's world, that only meant I'd sell my soul at a fixed price. I did not flatter myself that he saw me as an equal, but his respect was dangerous in its own way. Like a wolf respecting the fence around the sheep, right up until the day it didn't.

I finished the cleaning with an extra half-pint of carbolic, then set my brush aside and surveyed the work. Not perfect —nothing ever was, in this line—but good enough to fool a daytime eye. The stains in the mortar would linger, but only as a rumor, a faint bruise in the city's memory. I logged the time and the address in my little book, making a note about the knife's angle, the width of the splash, the oddity of a single button left in the gore.

A sound in the mist—footsteps? Or just my nerves? I stilled myself, forced my hand to stop shaking, and packed my tools with deliberate care. This was the part of the job I hated most: the walk back from the scene, with every shadow a possible tail, every alley's mouth a whispered threat.

Still better than the Coroner's Cart with Boyle.

Once I'd cross the bridge, I'd hire a hackney to take me back to Chelsea.

The fog was heavier now, pressing close as I turned up my collar and made for the main road. The streetlamps flickered, fighting a losing battle against the damp, and I tasted coal dust in every breath. In the silence, I reviewed my own inventory: blood cleaned, evidence logged, no fresh scars or curses to add to my record. A satisfactory evening, by any rational metric.

But as I walked, I could not shake the certainty that something had been watching me from that alley. Something not entirely human or perhaps simply more human than I cared to remember.

It was a feeling I'd grown used to. The only thing in this city more persistent than death was its memory.

I kept to the edge of the pavement, letting the night's fog blur me into just another shadow in a city rife with life and light. Past midnight, the river air was thick as gruel, sour with coal and human runoff. The respectable citizens had fled to their parlors and gin palaces, leaving the real London to its night terrors.

A crowd of pleasure-seekers spilled from a gambling den, the women shrieking with mock terror as a red-faced gent fumbled his way out, wallet emptied and dignity in tatters. Two urchins watched from the mouth of an alley, fingers itching, eyes sharp for easy prey. The younger one caught my stare and flinched, seeing (I suppose) a woman in black with the look of death about her, carrying a medical bag that reeked of formalin and secrets.

He nudged his mate, and they slunk back, melting into the mist.

I didn't know whether to be relieved or insulted.

I wasn't intimidating, was I? I was short, but not small. I was young, but not very. I was attractive, but not beautiful.

More than a few men have overlooked my overbite and spectacles in favor of my uncommonly red hair and, dare I confess, wider curves than are fashionable.

Still. I wasn't the sort to frighten children...Was I?

Maybe they could sense that I followed death around to clean up after him.

There were other watchers too. At the corner, a pair of constables stood guard, pointedly ignoring the queue at the brothel's private door—uniformed boys paid to keep up appearances, so long as the city's vices stayed in their proper lanes. A little farther down, a man in a velvet-collared coat waited by a lamplit cab, face in shadow, but I'd have bet my best scrubbing brush the scar on his cheek matched a description in Croft's old ledger.

The Hammer's men were everywhere, if you looked with the right eyes.

Sometimes I caught the gaze of women on the street— the bold ones, powdered and painted to outshine the filth, or the desperate ones, hair slicked down against the rain, and hope long since wrung out of them. They never looked for long. Some of them knew me by reputation, or by the sad parade of my former clients. A few still thought I was a kind of angel, albeit the sort who arrived too late.

The one who cleaned up their friend, their mother, or their husband.

I made the walk to Tite Street in thirteen minutes flat. Home was a lovely rowhouse indistinguishable from any other on the street. I let myself in with a practiced rattle of keys, tiptoeing around the slumbering form of Mary Jean McBride, my housekeeper, and her swaddled infant both asleep in the nook under the stairs.

The dear girl had waited up for me...

At least, she'd meant to.

Upstairs, the parlor lamp burned low, painting the walls

with the stuttering silhouettes of Aunt Nola's menagerie. Tarot cards were scattered across the table, along with crusts of soda bread and a thick pot of tea sat too long over the chafing. Aunt Nola herself dozed in the velvet armchair, wrapped in a shawl that once belonged to a Hungarian countess (according to her, at least), head sunk so low, I worried she'd finally gone over.

She roused at the sound of my bag hitting the desk. "Fiona," she said, voice reedy and muffled by sleep. "You're home."

"Just in time for dawn." I stripped off my gloves and poured a second cup of tea from the chipped pot. The taste was revolting, but I needed the lingering warmth and a bolt of energy.

"Was it a bad one tonight?" she asked, not looking up.

"They're all bad," I said, then softer: "But this was tidy, at least. No children. You should be in bed, Aunt Nola."

Aunt Nola grunted and pulled her shawl tighter around her nightgown. She fumbled for the deck of cards, fingers palsied but stubborn as ever. She never went to sleep without pulling the next day's fortune, as if the future could be persuaded by a bit of cardboard and willpower.

"Do you need a wash?" she asked. "You smell of vinegar and death."

"Well, that's a fine compliment for your kin," I said with mock impertinence but padded off to the scullery anyway, sluicing the city from my skin in the ice-cold sink. My hair, when I let it down, was a knotted frizz, and my spectacles sat askew on my nose.

I looked dreadful and couldn't bring myself to care.

I finished, dried off, and found Nola exactly where I'd left her, eyes closed, cards fanned across her lap. She snored faintly. On the table before her was the Three of Swords, stabbed clean through with pain, and the Fool, which she always insisted represented me. I took the cards, slipped them into her shawl, and kissed the top of her head.

I climbed to my own room.

It was cozier than the one I'd known back in County Waterford, yet it featured a large window offering a view of the rooftops, and an elegant mahogany writing desk adorned with neatly arranged letters, leather-bound ledgers, and a silver candelabra with partially burned candles. The desk was, as always, the first thing I checked.

There it was: a heavy cream envelope, sealed with the blue wax of the Tsadeq Syndicate. The wax was cracked, as if the messenger had thought better of being caught with it in the open. I turned it over in my fingers, weighing the odds of it being a simple payment versus another summons. If I'd learned anything from the Hammer, it was that the two were rarely separate.

I broke the seal. The letter inside was brief, in Roth's fine, deliberate hand:

Miss Mahoney—

Your services are required at the Velvet Glove before noon. Discretion is imperative. You will be compensated accordingly.

J

No signature, no elaborate threats, just the facts and a time. I should have felt honored, but instead I only felt tired. The Velvet Glove was not a place I relished visiting. Its reputation for discretion was matched only by its ability to make problems disappear—including, on occasion, the people who solved them.

I burned the letter over my candle, watched the paper curl into black lace, and ran mental inventory. My supplies were low, but I could make do. The real issue was not the job —it never was. The real issue was why the Hammer—Jorah—needed me, and why he needed me now.

I stared out the window for a minute, letting the city

speak. Out there, somewhere, Croft was awake and pacing. Out there, Night Horse was perhaps killing, or perhaps dead. Out there, the Ripper's legacy coiled in the stones, waiting for the next madman to make his name.

And in here, I was still myself, which was both comfort and curse.

I slept a handful of hours and rose to a noise from the parlor.

Aunt Nola, stirring.

I padded down to find her upright, eyes wild, cards strewn in a chaos of color.

"You're going out again," she said. Not a question.

"Only for a couple hours," I answered gently. "Can I help you to your bed?"

She jabbed a card at me: the Chariot, reversed. "You'll be forced to travel. There's danger in it. An answer in the grave. An enemy not born on this soil."

"Isn't there always?" I tried to smile. "You know these cards don't show you my future, Aunt Nola. Not really." They had been eerily correct several times, though I'd not deciphered thus until the dubious prediction was no longer helpful.

She shuffled another, held it up with trembling hands: the Moon, shrouded in clouds. "You won't unmask the truth. Not until it's too late."

"That's likely, knowing me." I knelt and kissed her cheek. "I'm due back before tea. Lock the doors, and don't let the teahouse boys in, even if they bring scones."

She gave a phlegmy laugh, and for a moment, I saw the aunt who'd once danced barefoot at wakes, who'd taught me that a woman could survive anything if she was stubborn enough.

At the threshold, I hesitated. The city was black and

endless. Somewhere out there, a fresh disaster waited with my name on it.

I gripped my bag, squared my shoulders, and stepped into the fog.

I didn't believe in omens.

But if there was an answer in the grave, I hoped it led me to Jack the Ripper.

Chapter Two

On paper, the Velvet Glove had a respectable address on the Strand where it bisects Wych St.

In practice, it was a gauntlet of every appetite and invention ever conceived by modern men. Gaslights burned day and night, throwing the shopfronts into perpetual theater. The banking halls and gentlemen's outfitters held the pavements with the same grim resolve as the ragged book-sellers and the bare-knuckle newsboys, each staking their claim to a few meters of the city's most expensive dirt.

It was all façade.

Whitewashed stone, preening columns, windows so clean they turned the morning into a mirror. The respectable world lived here, bustling even before noon: barristers in starched cravats, typists with their burden of secrets, shopgirls darting between errands like bright minnows in a current of black frockcoats.

The air tasted different, filtered through five stories of manners and money.

Blood spilled on this street, but it never seemed to stick.

The city's real stains ran east and south, where laundry lines were thicker than the fog and the gutters had names the maps wouldn't print. On the Strand, they sweep the night's debris away before the first tea tray hit the curb—out of sight, out of mind. But we denizens of the night knew better.

There were more types of vice here per furlong than in all the Gin Alleys of the East End.

The doorman, six feet of gristle beef in a livery better tailored than my best dress, gave me the same glance he always did, somewhere between a brotherly warning and a legitimate threat. "G'day, Miss Mahoney," he said, his accent a raw stew of the East End, not a lick of it genuine. "You're expected."

"Afternoon," I murmured, and flashed him a smile sharpened for occasions such as these. I patted the outside of my coat, fingers tracing the reassuring stiffness of the stiletto I kept sewn into the seam. It wasn't the kind of place to leave yourself to chance.

Inside, the Velvet Glove was built to disorient.

Every surface shimmered or glowed, from the mirrored columns to the murals of writhing cherubs licking each other's wounds. The lobby reeked of rose oil and cigar smoke, and above the din, some enterprising violinist sawed away at a Hungarian waltz as if the fate of Europe depended on it.

The gaming floor yawned ahead, a gilt swamp of high rollers and low intentions. Croupiers in starched collars manned the tables, flicking cards with the disdain of minor royalty, while the truly desperate haunted the periphery, hoping to catch a lucky windfall or at least the scent of one. I moved through it all like a rumor, attracting just enough attention to mark me as an oddity but not enough to become the afternoon's entertainment.

Halfway to the private stairs, I caught sight of the

"dames"—Jorah's word, not mine. They lined the wall by the far bar, gowns stitched so tight they looked poured on, faces lacquered to a high shine. The light from the chandelier made their powder glow faintly blue, like the lips of a drowning victim. One of them, a queen in peacock feathers, arched a perfect brow as I passed. I imagined what she'd say if she knew how often I'd seen her type laid out on a mortuary slab, skin just as flawless, eyes wide and unblinking. She offered a little laugh, brittle as eggshell.

"Look, ladies, it's death's chambermaid. You here to suck the blood off the Hammer's—"

"You're getting our professions mixed, my dear." I grimaced as if embarrassed for her. I'd nothing against her chosen profession, but I'd counter disrespect to mine.

The laugh curdled; she looked away. I kept walking, counting the number of eyes that trailed me.

More than usual.

I'd once infiltrated an upscale brothel not three blocks from the Velvet Glove to assist my friend, Amelia Croft, when the prostitutes she sewed for had been picked off by a killer. If that case had taught me anything, it was that women could be every bit as vicious as men, but our warfare is more subtle.

Less collateral damage.

Due to the experience, I now employed my sharp tongue more judiciously and with greater effect.

Two of Roth's security men had positioned themselves in the old checkerboard pattern: one at the base of the stairs, the other at the top, both with hands folded as if in prayer. I recognized the nearer one—bruiser named Krazinski, once rumored to have chewed off a man's thumb in a betting dispute. He inclined his head, not a nod but an invitation.

"Miss Mahoney. He's waitin'."

"I'd hate to disappoint," I said, mounting the first step. Krazinski fell in a half-pace behind.

Upstairs, the corridor pulsed with muffled laughter and the clink of glass. At each door, a little tableau: some discreet assignation, a stifled argument, the exchange of something more precious than coin. Roth's people were everywhere, but I knew better than to look for them. They'd find you if they wanted you, and if you weren't wanted...

You'd never see them coming.

The Hammer's sanctum was on the third floor, far above the noise and clamor, tucked behind a stretch of hallway so plush it made the Queen's own apartments look like a parish workhouse. The walls here were covered in brocaded silk, the kind that sucked in sound and made even a gunshot seem like a polite cough.

At the end of the corridor, the guard stopped before a mahogany door so glossy it gave a warped reflection of my own face: pale, freckled, red hair barely tamed by a tortoise-shell comb. I smoothed my coat, more out of habit than pride, and prepared my best funeral-parlor smile at the guards flanking the entry like chessmen.

One rapped three times, the knocks so precisely spaced I half expected a Morse code message. The door opened on a whisper, and Krazinski gestured me inside.

I paused just outside the threshold, letting my eyes adjust to the dark. The air tasted of old books and sweet smoke, an improvement on the main floor.

Roth's office was a study in contrasts. The lighting was soft and gold, glowing from a chandelier designed to resemble an inverted crown of thorns. It cast long shadows on the collection of rare books lining the walls, every spine a little monument to the pursuit of forbidden knowledge. Behind the Hammer's desk, a stained-glass window glowed with the city's meager light, casting ribbons of crimson and blue over the desk's lacquered surface and, by extension, over the man himself.

I counted to three, then stepped in, shutting the door behind me. The old Irish saying about stepping into the Devil's parlor came to mind, but I doubted even the Devil had Jorah's taste in expensive carpets.

He sat as if he'd been sculpted there: hands folded, posture so erect it bordered on parody, a frozen silhouette as sharp and mathematical as a Da Vinci. Only his eyes ruined the illusion of marble—they glittered, alive and always hungry.

"Fiona," he said, and his voice was a knife wrapped in velvet. "Punctual as ever. London could set its clocks by you."

"I'll only be tardy to my own execution," I replied, matching his smile with one of my own. "But I suppose you're one for the element of surprise."

The Hammer was less a man than a force of nature in bespoke tailoring. Indeed, he was the only man I'd ever met who could make a three-piece suit into a weapon more lethal than a garrote. Today, he was arrayed in slate and sapphire, every line on his body calculated for maximum intimidation, but not a single crease out of place. He wore his hair in the new style—close-cropped, parted with surgical precision—his pale, angular face almost luminous in the lamplight, cheekbones and jaw so severe they cast their own shadows.

He moved behind the desk with the careful, deliberate grace of a man who'd been taught from infancy to never waste a gesture. He motioned to the cut-glass decanter, heavy with cognac. "Even the unexpected can be prepared for, with the right tools. Drink?"

I considered it, weighing the risks, then shook my head. "I prefer my poisons measured...and not before midday."

Jorah let out a breath that might have been a laugh, pouring himself a modest finger anyway. "A wise choice."

The figure in the corner—a strawberry-haired woman in a high-collared dark dress remained utterly still, hands folded in her lap. She was younger than I, but only just, her features more elegant and her freckles more prominent.

"I see you've acquired a new...employee," I said, glancing her way.

Jorah followed my gaze, the smile never wavering. "A companion for the evening. She hears nothing, says less. Consider her an ornament."

I doubted that. In the Glove, everyone was listening, even the wallpaper.

"I could never consider a human being ornamental," I said, unmistakable meaning lacing my voice with censure. I tried not to notice his ornament favored me more than a little.

I didn't miss the way the companion stiffened. It wasn't often someone spoke to the Hammer with anything but deference. But I'd saved his life more than once, and I did an exemplary job of washing the blood he spilled from the streets he claimed to own. I did fear that one day this man might be the architect of my demise, but not today.

He lifted the glass to his lips but didn't drink. "I understand you had a difficult evening."

"Nothing a hot bath and a lobotomy wouldn't cure."

A wicked smile. "Avoiding Whitechapel these days, are you?"

I didn't bother answering. If Roth wanted details, he already had them. The Glove's network of informants was legendary, and there wasn't a parish in London that didn't have a debt to settle with Roth's silent partners in the global organization that was the Tsadeq Syndicate.

"Why am I here?" I asked. "What's the nature of the job?"

He set the glass down, fingers making a cathedral of themselves. "I'll not waste your time. There's a situation in

Witcombe Green—three exhumations in as many weeks. Bodies left in rather...inventive states of disrepair. Our friends in the Syndicate wish the problem handled with discretion and, more importantly, deniability."

I said nothing. When men like Roth gave you the facts, you listened for the spaces between them.

"The police are out of their depth," he continued. "And I'd not like to rouse Scotland Yard, but they're more accustomed to drunken brawls than ritual desecration. And the press—" Here, a flash of teeth. "The press always hungers for a new Ripper. I'd not want my people to become sensationalized in another byline."

His people. The Jews.

"And what makes you think I can do anything the police haven't?"

"You're a cleaner, Miss Mahoney. But more importantly, you're an observer. You see what others ignore, the patterns and inconsistencies. You ask the dangerous questions."

I didn't bother with false modesty. "Maybe I'm just cursed to attract the attention of murderers, Mr. Roth. Perhaps I'm just the one Irish unlucky enough to work for both you lot and the police, which is a balancing act I wouldn't wish on the circus."

That drew a genuine laugh, low and rumbling. "You see? This is why you're so valuable. You possess both insight and immunity to sentimentality. The other trades—police, doctors, even the clergy—they bring their own baggage. You only bring the tools required, and you are ruthlessly efficient."

There was a compliment in there, somewhere.

I'd plenty of baggage and we both knew it.

"What happened at Witcombe Green that I can help with?" I asked.

He steepled his fingers. "Each corpse belonged to a notable member of the Jewish community—an alderman, a rabbi, a financier. The bodies were left at the doorsteps of Russian or Jewish émigrés and old-money families. Someone is trying to send a message, but the meaning is...obscure."

"Or too obvious," I said, "and you're hoping I'll tell you it isn't what it looks like."

He smiled again, and this time it was almost warm. "I have faith in your objectivity."

"Why can't you send someone of your—er—people to inspect? I don't know enough about Judaism to see the nuances."

"Yes, but if a syndicate member investigates, lips will cork faster than a gin jar in a raid."

I watched him for a long moment, letting the silence stretch. He could hold a silence better than any corpse I'd ever met.

Finally, he leaned back, picking up the glass and swirling the contents. "Also, since the bodies have been exhumed once a week for three consecutive weeks, I want you installed there when the fourth one makes its ghastly appearance." He took a drink, regarding me over the rim of his glass, and I tried very hard not to watch the muscles in his throat work over the collar.

"Can you not just pay off a coroner to be there?" I asked. "I'm not possessed of the training—"

"You've contacts in that regard," he cut me off. "Your tutelage of Dr. Phillips, for example. And you've toyed about with enough death to analyze what's out of ordinary."

"That's debatable if it's—"

"The address is in the envelope," he said, tossing it in front of me with an ominous weight. "So is a retainer, in case you find yourself in need of, shall we say, expedited removal or have unexpected expenses. The rest will be given upon completion of the task. I'll have a man placed nearby if you require assistance, but I know you prefer to work alone."

I took the envelope, resisting the urge to open it then and there.

"Anything else?" I asked.

He drained the glass, set it down with surgical precision. "Only this: If you find the author of our little drama, avoid showing them the courtesy of a warning. There are lines even my associates prefer not to cross, and I would hate to see your name added to a list better left unwritten."

It was the gentlest threat I'd ever heard from Roth.

I stood, tucking the envelope away.

"If you want deniability," I said, "maybe try not sending the Irish woman with the blood under her fingernails. People notice."

He didn't answer, but the look in his eye suggested that was the whole point.

I let that sit, feeling the burn of curiosity and something darker. The pattern in the crimes was unmistakable—a calling card, deliberate and cold. I thought of the button in my pocket, of Mary Kelly, of how the city always found new ways to remind you nothing stayed buried forever.

"Surely you have some private investigator who would be proficient at this. Again, why me?"

"A question I hear often," he said with a secret smile. "But since you've come into my employment—"

"Since I was conscripted, you mean," I corrected, reminding him that I'd taken one job from him early in my career before I'd realized with which devil I'd just made a deal.

"You've proven your analytical prowess." He smiled, broad this time, the teeth just a shade too white. "In return, I'll see to it that your aunt remains comfortable and out of the asylum; you've received a modest fortune for your trouble. And, your debt to the Syndicate will be considered paid in full."

"I've never had a debt to the—"

"Understand that means they—we—will no longer call upon your services unless you've offered them of your own accord."

Stunned, I considered his proposition. In this city, everyone worked for someone else. Even I, who owned my own business, still answered to the reaper.

Jorah was many things. A gangster. A flesh-peddler. A bookmaker. A powerful ally and a terrifying enemy.

But he kept his word and paid his debts.

And I knew most people didn't get out from under the Syndicate's eye in anything but a pine box.

He was handing me a gift he knew I longed for.

I nodded, glancing once more at the woman in the shadows. She watched me with dead eyes, unblinking. In the life I'd planned with Mary Kelly, I could have very easily been in her position.

Jack the Ripper had forged me a new destiny by what he'd done to Mary.

I'd never thank him for it.

I buttoned my coat against the thought. "I'll need a carriage."

"Of course," said Roth, and gestured to Krazinski, who reappeared with the efficiency of a well-tuned trap. "Take Miss Mahoney wherever she requires."

Krazinski inclined his head, but not before I caught the glint of a smile—respect, or maybe a warning.

I left him there, in the golden dark. At the door, I looked back just once, and found him already buried in paperwork, his face aglow in the red and blue of the stained glass.

His companion's gaze felt like a knife in my back.

The corridor outside was silent, the only sound my own footsteps. The fog had seeped in through the cracks of the old building, blurring the lines between memory and dread.

At the street, I paused again, looking up at the lights of the Glove. They burned all night, as if to mock the darkness that gathered in the city's bones.

I wondered, not for the first time, if a man like Jorah Roth ever saw his own reflection, or if he'd learned long ago to ignore it.

Chapter Three

There was a peculiar sort of humility in traveling first class by train.

You paid double to be left alone, then spent the entire journey marveling at how much more efficiently the world catered to the needs of its wealthy. The seats were broad and cushioned, the tea never stewed, and the windows were so clean you could stage an autopsy on them, should the mood strike.

I stretched my boots on the lush blue carpet of the private compartment, marveling at the waste of it all. Roth's "retainer"—crisp enough to cut a finger—sat on the little fold-out table alongside my notebook foolscap paper each marked with the kind of neat, impersonal hand that might as well have been set in type.

Victims.

All deceased men over forty. All of them Jews. Two of them with life-long ties to the Syndicate and one with no tie at all...

The first had been an alderman, philanthropist and—

apparently—Syndicate member: Joshua Wertheim, late of Buckinghamshire. Died peacefully of heart trouble, or so the local quack said. He'd used his status to file or falsify documents with the English government for the Syndicate and had close ties with Former Prime Minister Disraeli. Three weeks after burial, someone dug him up, pried out his teeth, and left the body on the doorstep of a wealthy Russian tobacconist with a note:

For your expensive collection, Sir. Enjoy.

The second was a rabbi, Samuel Bernstein, gone two months before similarly exhumed. No teeth this time, but all the fingers clipped off at the second knuckle. Even I had to shudder in revulsion at the thought of a corpse two months rotten. I wondered what solutions and chemicals they used on the stoop of the Goldsmid estate upon which he was discarded. The smell would have sunk into the very stones.

The third was recent: a financier of some repute named Jacob Auerbach, believed to have passed away naturally and interred less than a week ago. However, when they'd found him at the Goldsmid estate, they discovered a horrifying truth. His body lay like a crucifixion victim, mouth stuffed with shreds of a racy tabloid. It became immediately obvious Mr. Auerbach hadn't died of natural causes, but of three very deep stabs with a very large blade. The wounds told a clear story: each penetration delivered with surgical precision, left to right across the abdomen, the final one piercing his heart.

I tapped my pen on the foolscap, wondering what kind of idiot would try to pass off a fresh murder as an elaborate grave-robbing stunt. Someone with more taste for spectacle than subtlety, that much was obvious. But the thing that bothered me, truly, was the second page of notes—the one from Roth himself, with the oblique references to "broader patterns" and "implications for the Syndicate's interests." Jorah Roth didn't waste his time on necrophiliac pranks unless there was something at stake for him personally or professionally.

And that, even more than the imagined stench of the decomposed Rabbi, set my teeth on edge.

The train lurched, throwing my carefully sorted notes onto the floor. I stooped to retrieve them, cursing the false promise of luxury as the tea threatened to slosh onto my skirt. The skirt itself was not what anyone would call delicate. For traveling it was well-tailored boiled wool, charcoal black, hemmed at mid-ankle to facilitate rushing, with secret pockets sewn on the inside for keys, evidence bags, or, in a pinch, brass knuckles. My blouse was fine, but plain, and I'd kept my hair pinned in a severe bun and understated cap with a lonely raven feather, partly to avoid being mistaken for one of the companion girls that haunted the better train cars.

Men had an aversion to the word *no* on a good day. It got worse when they traveled.

Practicality over beauty was my general Modus Operandi. I wasn't above silken undergarments and fashionable cuts, but a gown didn't last long in my line work. Still, I made a point to check my reflection in the window, a habit that was less vanity and more the need to confirm I remained physically present in the world.

Through the glass, the city's edge faded into shanties, brickworks, and then fields as the train accelerated north. The fog pursued us like a hell hound, thinning only slightly as we rattled into the open country.

The periodical pauses at a handful of stations went by without note until we ground to a stop on a platform so rural, I'd have blinked and missed it. The porter informed me it was "a matter of the line" and suggested we'd be at least half an hour. When he'd retreated, I rose and decided to stretch my legs, if only to satisfy the old itch of freedom that came from being neither watched nor required.

The early summer air on the platform was chilly and tasted of wet straw, a lovely reprieve from the coal smog that haunted every breath in London. The station itself was deserted but for a single lamp, its glow shivering in the morning mist. Beyond the low fence, a row of trees—black, leafless, arthritic—stood in mute accusation against the sodden sky. I paced the length of the platform, the gravel crunching under my boots, and felt the strange presence of possibility: no police, no employers, no dead to see to, only the simple question of what might come next.

A crow perched on the station sign, glaring at me with an intelligence I found more honest than most men. I considered, for a moment, the logic of the current case. Three bodies, three depositions, all staged for maximum humiliation and minimal effect.

What was the point?

All three victims had two things in common. Buckinghamshire as their residence, Jerusalem their ancestral homeland.

So, the likely motive for such heinous pranks would be either personal or ethnically prejudicial.

That was what I needed to find out first, then perhaps I could do something before another body was exhumed. Jorah seemed confident one would be.

For the multitude of reasons one could imagine, I preferred a corpse to be new when I cleaned.

The wind changed, and with it came the sharp, iron scent of something animal. It wasn't unpleasant, just undeniably vital, the kind of smell you got only when the blood was still fresh and the world was waiting to see what would be made of it. I wondered if I'd ever known such vitality, or if I'd spent too much of my life sorting the dead to recognize it.

The train whistled its warning to leave the moment I

spied the shadow of a predator disappearing into the dark tree line.

With blood on the wind...it was best I returned to the train.

As I walked, I cataloged the station in the same way I'd cataloged hundreds of crime scenes: the wet boot prints on the slates, the smear of grease on the handrail, the delicate crust of old bird droppings on the bench.

I noticed things others tried not to, I realized, unsure of what to do with that information.

It certainly didn't make one more popular among their peers.

Before stepping up into the railcar, I paused to look once more at the line of trees. They seemed to lean closer now, as if listening. I resisted the urge to salute the crow and instead returned to my compartment, closing the door behind me.

The luxury felt more suffocating now, the air heavy with the floral perfume of the cleaning crew and the faint, sweet scent of pipe tobacco from a neighboring car.

I entered my compartment on the return, expecting only the musty perfume of unwashed velvet and the echo of my own footsteps.

Instead, I found Aramis Night Horse seated in my place, hands folded with the kind of severe, reptilian stillness that made you wish he would just move—shout, break something, *anything* to crack the tension and malicious danger that billowed around him like black powder smoke.

Jorah Roth was known as the Hammer in London, and Aramis Night Horse was the Blade.

It had been months. Longer, if you counted in the emotional arithmetic that dogged my waking hours, since I'd seen him, and everything I imagined I'd say dispelled like a morning fog.

I stopped, one hand braced on the doorframe, the other

clutching my case so tight the old cut on my palm split open again, a neat little bead of blood joining the list of indignities.

His eyes—those bastard, bottomless eyes—tracked the motion with interest but not concern.

"Fiona." His voice hadn't changed. It was still low, rough-edged, blunted by an American patois and the whisper of a native language I'd never begin to recognize.

"Mr. Night Horse." I uttered his name with a veneer of detachment, as if we were mere acquaintances and not two people who had shared a night so passionate it haunted me.

It wasn't the only ghost we shared.

He'd also plunged a blade into Aidan Fitzpatrick, the man who had been my sole guide in the bewildering landscape of love...until he'd been caught out as a war criminal and a ritual killer.

It was this dichotomy of memory—the paradox of arousal and acrimony—that painted every interaction with Aramis Night Horse in shades of gray.

He wore expensively tailored clothes that seemed almost scandalously out of place on his chiseled frame, like a beautiful mistake. A white linen shirt clung to his torso beneath a brocade vest, collarless with sleeves meticulously rolled to reveal muscled forearms. No jewelry adorned him, no insignia claimed his allegiance, but the confident bulge under his jacket hinted at a knife, and another, smaller blade was discreetly stitched with precision at the seam of his left boot.

For a moment neither of us spoke. The silence stretched, taut as the wire in a garrote, until I realized I was the one refusing to let go of the door.

I shut it with more force than needed, aching to give my hands something to do that wasn't reach across the table and grab him by the throat—or, worse, by the lapels, and drag him in for a kiss so brief and savage it would cost us both a week of nightmares. I set my case on the bench opposite and sat, fussed with my skirt, anything to keep the tremor in my hands from becoming visible.

He smiled, or at least arranged his mouth in a way that suggested the rumor of a smile. "You look well."

"You don't," I said with a droll sigh, though it wasn't strictly true.

Night Horse looked exactly as he always had. Cruel, cynical, coiled, every muscle in a state of low-key readiness like a wolf that had learned to thrive on starvation. His hair was longer, the black rope of it pulled low at the nape, but his face still bore the same severe, angular geometry I'd both feared and hated...then desired. The only new feature was a thin white scar running from his left temple to the tip of his ear.

It shouldn't have made him even handsomer. More compelling to look at.

Lord, help me, but it did.

"Are you on your own errand for the Hammer?" I asked tartly, "or has he sent you to keep me honest?"

No answer. Just a narrowing of the eyes, as if searching for evidence of rot in my soul.

I pulled off my gloves, finger by finger, watching him watch me. I checked the cut on my finger, grateful not to see blood.

The trembling was slight but there, and I hated him for seeing it.

"Or am I to intuit that you came on your own accord," I said, busying myself with the papers on the table.

"I'm here to protect the...interests of the Syndicate. To make sure all is clean and quiet. Nothing else."

Something like soft hope turned sour in my heart.

I remembered then, with hideous clarity, how we'd left it. Not with a declaration, not even a goodbye, just a mutual understanding that our lives were shaped by violence, and the only thing waiting for us at the end was...more violence.

We'd turned to each other with a powerful need to offset the horrors of it all with a few hours of pleasure in the dark. He'd said, "This isn't for keeping," and I'd agreed, but later, whilst drunk and lonely in my own home, I realized I'd *wanted* it kept, just for a little while longer.

"Clean?!" I scoffed. "I've never seen you scrub up after yourself. That's always my job. I trust I won't be considered a mess in need of your particular sort of cleaning."

Night Horse didn't smile, but his posture eased, just a fraction. "Foresight is not among my skills, Fiona."

"Fair enough," I clipped, sealing my lips together. If he wanted to be infuriatingly silent, I could as well. One would assume one could ask a former lover to provide a simple promise not to murder one, but when that lover was London's most lethal assassin...

Apparently, one couldn't expect too much.

I made a show of reviewing the notes, but my attention flicked between the words and the man before me. I wanted to ask where he'd been these past months, who he'd killed...

Why he still haunted my dreams.

Instead, I said, "You'll want to see the sites, then. A tobacconist and the Goldsmid estate. I'm wondering if I should make a visit to the cemetery."

"I'll go where you go," he replied. There was nothing flirtatious in it; it was a statement of fact, an order received and internalized.

"Is that so?" I said, letting the sarcasm drip from my tongue. "What's the plan, then? You shadow me through the —investigation—then report back to the Hammer?"

"We will both do what we are paid by Roth to do." He looked out the window, dismissing the subject. The countryside flashed by, punctuated by the dark shapes of grazing sheep, and for a second, he looked like a child at a loss for what to do with freedom. "The same as always."

Those words fogged the window with a hint of discontent.

It would be easy to say that I didn't care, that his presence was as meaningful to me as the weather or the quality of the rail service. But the truth was, my pulse was so loud in my ears I half-expected it to leave a bruise on my neck.

He had been, after all, my first lover.

And the man who'd slid his lethal blade into my first love.

Granted, the "love" in question had been a monster I never recognized, but that didn't make it simpler.

Or easier to forget.

Our last time together was a muddle of longing and self-loathing, a scandalous secret I barely admitted even to myself. An act of rebellion against a society who would own all my decisions and hand them to a man.

And against the Ripper. Who demanded in a letter I stay pure or else incur his wrath.

He did not own my body.

But Night Horse had for several unforgettable hours... And I'd give it back to him if he asked for it.

The train juddered, slowing as it approached another nameless town. For a moment, we rode in silence, the rhythm of the rails a metronome for our mutual uncertainty.

At last, he said, "You've changed."

I imagined he implied that he wasn't used to my silence.

"So have you," I replied, biting down on my lips so as not to give him the satisfaction of another syllable he didn't earn.

He opened his mouth, as if to say something important when the door to the compartment slid open before either of us could speak, a woman entered.

"Is zis her?" she asked in a dramatically French accent as her dark, sultry eyes cataloged everything in two long sweeps of my person. "I've been aching for this moment, Miss Mahoney. The extraordinary woman who finds the truth in the blood of the slain. I am Celeste Beaumont who is both enchanted and honored to meet you."

I blinked once before I could breathe.

Twice before I could register that I detested the way my surname sounded in her accent. Mah-Oh-ni.

She was so sharply dressed she made the velvet upholstery seem like sackcloth. I unkindly decided she looked like the kind of woman who never tripped, never sweated, never tore her stockings on the twisted spines of city cobbles. The French, I was told, considered grace a basic civil right. Celeste Beaumont—who now occupied a full third of my compartment—wore her striking beauty the way a cardinal wore red: as a uniform, and as a warning. Her coat was fawn-colored, tightly fitted, and fastened with lacquered buttons. Her hat was a modest feathered pillbox, but the way she inclined it made you forget it wasn't a crown. She carried herself with the assurance of someone who had only ever traveled in first class, and who'd never in her life been forced to check the soles of her shoes for horse dung before entering a room.

"Fiona...please call me Fiona," I stuttered as she bent to place two very close kisses on each of my cheeks. She smelled like a cherry orchard. "Can we erm...help you?"

She sat next to Night Horse and, after a perfunctory greeting in French, placed one hand on his arm. The gesture was neither possessive nor affectionate...per se. More like a person staking a flag in an inhospitable patch of land and daring the elements to try and reclaim it.

Was she—with him?

He barely glanced at her but the shift in his body language was immediate. Some tension eased, as though the presence of this woman resolved an unspoken question.

"Fiona," said Celeste, "I hope you don't mind if we share

the compartment. There is little privacy on these lines, and we have much to discuss."

"Do we?" I asked in genuine confusion.

"Aramis, you did not tell her?" She imitated a slap on his knuckles.

Aramis?

I'd known the man a handful of years and never in my *life* had even Jorah—who'd given me leave to use his own name when in our own company—called the Blade anything but said moniker or his tribal surname, such as it was.

And here Celeste Beaumont was touching him as blithely as she pleased.

Calling him *Aramis*...

Sourly, I searched his face for any clues as to their connection and, as per usual, he gave none.

"Am I to understand you're investigating the same case...?"

Her laughter bubbled out of a throat so pale and pretty I was momentarily transfixed.

"Darling, a woman like me doesn't get her hands dirty, nor does she involve herself in the affairs of wicked men." She scrunched her nose up at Night Horse as if he'd been a scamp. "My only function for you is as a key."

I blinked again, hating how confused I always seemed to be in the presence of Night Horse.

Aramis?

I hoped I hid my flinch every time she said it.

Celeste apparently found my bemusement a delight, and she covered her mouth as she giggled. "I open doors," she explained as if delivering a clever line to a joke. "I'm an esteemed guest of the Goldsmid estate for the midsummer faire, as I'm being courted by Lord and Lady Vronsky's son, Alexei. I'm in need of a lady's maid and companion along with my own groomsman." She set about removing her gloves with an efficiency that made my own method look childish. She crossed her legs at the ankle, which in any other woman would have looked demure, but with Celeste seemed like a calculated insult to Victorian restraint.

"I am told you are the finest cleaner in the city," she began, "and also the sharpest mind in matters of...unconventional deaths."

I considered correcting her, then decided I liked the ambiguity. "I do my best," I said. "Though I'm no detective. Certainly not anyone of note."

"Nonsense! You are known in the most interesting of circles as a brave and brilliant woman."

I was?

Celeste clapped her hands once, becoming dramatically conspiratorial though we had no eavesdroppers. "Now, we must discuss the ghastly matter at hand."

She reached into her bag—an absurdly expensive thing, leather soft as meringue—and pulled out a sheaf of papers, each marked in the same careful hand as the ones from Roth. She laid them on the table with the gravity of a lawyer presenting evidence. Night Horse did not move, did not speak, just watched us both with the predatory calm of a cat confronted with two canaries and no dietary restrictions.

"As I told you, I'm staying with a cousin of my mothers, the Goldsmids, while being courted by the Vronsky heir, Alexei." She leaned over to conspire with me, as a woman, I thought. "He's conveyed the intention to propose during this festival holiday, but that was before all this...bother." She waved away three dead bodies as if they were an inconvenience to her upcoming nuptials. "It behooves you and Night Horse to have ready access to both estates, and I'm in a position to provide that." She giggled and tapped her fan on Night Horse's shoulder. "It gives me a chance to repay a debt."

I blinked. "That's...bold."

"It's necessary," Celeste replied. "No one would question a lady's companion, and I require someone who can both blend in and observe. I would do it myself, but as you see, I am not suited to subterfuge."

She was at least that self-aware.

"I don't suppose I'll have to curtsy to you," I said, searching for the catch.

She considered it. "No! It's considered the new thing to pay your lady's maid to be your chaperone or companion. It's more enjoyable and convivial. But mostly, you will stand behind me, fetch things, and generally do what I ask. Can you manage?"

"Easy enough," I said, hiding my doubt with a shrug.

I didn't miss the ghost of mirth hovering around Night Horse's lips.

Nor did I appreciate it.

"There is more," she went on, her tone shifting from businesslike to something softer. "There will be people at this event who do not wish for outsiders to know the truth of these deaths. You must be careful what you say and to whom. I have arranged for you to stay in a small annex next to my rooms if you find that acceptable."

I glanced at Night Horse, expecting him to weigh in.

He didn't.

"It's acceptable," I said. "Though I warn you, I'm not much good at hairdressing."

"I did not expect that you were, darling," she said, and flashed that quick, irrepressible smile that made me wonder if I'd just been complimented or insulted.

A silence settled. For a few minutes we watched the world scroll by, each lost in our own calculations. I tried to imagine the kind of person who could pull off a triple exhumation, stage the remains with such flair, then bait a woman like

Celeste into the open. Whoever they were, I hoped they had a taste for disappointment.

At last, I said, "How do you know Mr. Night Horse?"

She didn't bristle, didn't pause. "He saved my life once, in Paris. Since then, I have looked out for him, and he for me."

It was the closest thing to sentimentality I'd ever heard in regards to Night Horse, and it made my heart ache in a way I hadn't prepared for.

Enough not to ask follow-up questions.

Paris? Was that where Night Horse had been these last months?

The train shuddered as it crossed a junction, and for a moment, the lights flickered. When they steadied, Celeste was regarding me with a new expression: not suspicion, but appraisal, as if trying to decide whether to trust me with a secret or a loaded pistol.

She leaned in, dropping her voice. "You are brave, Miss Mahoney. But I fear you may not be careful enough."

I gave her the best smile I could manage. "If I was careful, I wouldn't be on this train."

She laughed then, a sound that was as much challenge as it was delight, and I decided I liked her—even if I did suspect she and Night Horse had once, or perhaps still, shared more than intelligence.

"What is it that you do, Miss Beaumont?" Who was she to be courting infamous Russian nobility?

"As little as possible," she said cryptically, extracting a long cigarette holder and a silver case.

I looked out the window so she didn't catch my outrage. Two people incapable of answering a question in good faith. This was going to be a longer trip than I'd accounted for.

As the train neared Witcombe Green, the sky darkened, and a new fog gathered outside, thicker and more persistent than the last. The compartment door shivered once as the train took a corner, and I caught my reflection again. The eyes looking back were sharp, watchful, and—though I'd never admit it—hungry for the challenge.

I watched the countryside unspool, field by field, and wondered who would be waiting for me at the end of the line. If Roth was right, the answer would be nothing good.

But perhaps, for once, it would be something I could understand.

Chapter Four

T here was a quality to the stormy light in rural train stations, an unkindness, really, that painted even the healthiest souls into specters.

I recognized at once, before the train had even fully braked, that the rangy, hunched figure waiting on the platform was neither friend nor well-wisher. He radiated the determined, restless energy of a man who expected to be seen, and who feared being noticed.

I pulled my things together and followed Celeste onto the gravel and boards, filling my lungs with the afternoon Buckinghamshire atmosphere, a freshening drizzle that threatened to soak expectations before arrival.

Night Horse stepped off last, surveying the platform with the alertness of a wolf in an unfamiliar forest.

The station itself was a quaint, elegantly designed pavilion, its graceful architecture adorned with intricate woodwork and a polished, expansive platform that gleamed under the soft glow of ornate lampposts. Beyond the gentle illumination, the fields disappeared into a delicate mist, casting a serene and mysterious allure over the landscape.

"The wealthy milled in camphor-scented wool. The women rushed beneath umbrellas, dragging their shivering children while soaking porters protected their luggage."

Even the mud was more discerning than I.

The wind took on a raw edge, the sort that scraped the lungs clean and sharpened the tongue. The three of us made for a strange party, even in a world where every traveling party was, by default, a nest of secrets. Celeste was inscrutable, but her confidence bespoke years spent in rooms where her beauty was the only currency required.

Night Horse was another thing entirely: too silent, too still, and yet carrying a violence so palpable that even the crows at the edge of the garden refused to caw.

As for myself, I looked every inch the undertaker's errand girl, with my serviceable skirt, sensible boots, and the red hair knotted so tight it might have required a scalpel to undo.

There was no mistaking me for a lady, and I was fine with that.

So trapped in my observations was I, that I barely noticed the figure draw near, revealing himself.

I immediately cringed as I recognized the masculine features.

Not an enemy, but certainly not an ally.

Daniel Hartwell, a London journalist as hungry a parasite as ever drained the blood from a city's scandals. I'd seen him hound detectives and victims in a most ungainly manner, though his articles were more widely read than the letters from the Queen.

He evoked a professor in a tweed coat, and his sand-colored hair—so carefully unkempt—marked him as both a professional observer and an aspiring subject. He grinned as if he'd been waiting his entire life for this moment.

"Miss Fiona Mahoney," he said, voice pitched for maximum resonance in the damp. "What a fortuitous coincidence! I was just reading your name on the passenger manifest before we disembarked."

Celeste, who'd barely taken in the scene, now fixed Hartwell with a look so arch it could have supported a bridge. "Do we know you, sir?"

Hartwell affected a bow. "Daniel Hartwell, The Telegraph. Investigative desk."

Celeste gave a brittle laugh. "A smile like that is wasted on a gossip hound." Another one of her remarks that left the listener wondering if she'd meant to caress or sting.

Night Horse cut between them, not quite blocking the path, but making it clear there were easier people to inconvenience on this platform. "We are expected elsewhere," he said, and his American accent made the phrase sound like a loaded pistol.

"Yes, yes, of course," Hartwell said, stepping back with a show of humility. "But I would be remiss in my duties if I did not ask—are you here in connection with the unfortunate events at the Goldsmid estate last week?"

Celeste sniffed, pretending not to hear him. "Is there a porter for these bags?" She looked around, aghast at the lack of infrastructure. "We are not expected to drag our own trunks about like peasants, are we?"

Her trunk, I observed, was conspicuously absent. Only the porters' handcart and a few smaller parcels made it onto the platform. Celeste wheeled around in a fury, her composure dissolving at the prospect of being separated from her wardrobe. "Where is my trunk? I distinctly labeled it and paid for priority removal."

A porter in a hat three sizes too large approached, already sweating with the effort of dealing with his betters. "There's been a, ah, delay on the goods carriage, madam. We're addressing it, but it may be a half-hour."

Celeste's eyes narrowed to razors. "Completely unacceptable. I'll have a word with your station master. Aramis, will you be a darling and assist?"

Night Horse nodded looking neither anticipatory or aggrieved, and the pair stalked toward the station office, leaving me alone on the platform with Daniel Hartwell and the mist.

I watched their retreat with both amusement and envy. There was a certain pleasure in seeing someone who was used to having her way denied it, even if only by a malfunction of the rural supply chain.

When they were out of earshot, Hartwell sidled closer, lowering his voice. "I'll be frank, Miss Mahoney. I'm not here to pester you, merely to observe. There's a story brewing up here that's set half the Home Office on edge."

I gave him nothing but a raised brow in silent calculation of how fast I could push him under the next train.

There were only three types of journalists in London: the hacks, the barracudas, and the suicidally persistent. Hartwell was cut from the third cloth—lean, wind-chapped, with a vital energy that bordered on manic and brain working faster than the average man. "You've no business with me, Hartwell. Go peddle your conspiracy to the drunks on the southbound."

He didn't flinch. "Conspiracies are the only thing worth reading these days. That, and the obituaries, which is where I usually find your name—buried, but there all the same."

A less charitable person might have hit him. Instead, I adopted a look I hoped as withering as Celeste's, letting the silence settle like silt in a river.

"I've made your business my business. Two corpses in Lambeth, one in Bow." He leaned closer, voice dropping to a whisper. "Is it true the body was left on the steps? And that it was missing...pieces?"

"The details aren't for print."

"Oh, but they are," he said, and in that moment, I saw the animating spirit of every ghoul who ever made their fortune on other people's misery. "You're here to clean up the Goldsmid mess, aren't you?"

"Goldsmid," I repeated, keeping my tone flat. "Never heard the name."

He rolled his eyes. "You're a terrible liar, Mahoney. Everyone knows the Goldsmid estate's the epicenter. The exhumations, the anonymous letters, the parade of Russian 'guests' every night. You think London can't smell a political scandal even up here?"

I scoffed. "I think London can't smell much beyond its own sewers, and I count journalists like you among the worst of its stenches."

He grinned, undeterred. "The Telegraph's running a feature on ritual crimes in the East End and beyond. There are criminal exhumations in town, as well, and I'm looking for a link. I thought you might like to offer some professional insight."

"Print this, then: anyone who reads your tripe is either an idiot or a masochist." I turned away, but he followed, close enough that I could feel the heat of his body through the cold.

"Are these exhumations anti-Semitic?" he persisted. "Or just another way of keeping the immigrants in their place?"

The question landed, sharper than expected. "Ask your own paper's publisher. He's got more opinions on Jews and Irish than he has on politics."

Hartwell's eyes narrowed. "He's not just at the Jews, is he? Russians, Poles, Chinese, everyone. There's something here that doesn't fit the usual narrative. And you, Miss Mahoney—you're the only one who ever walks away from these scenes with the story straight. You're not afraid to see things as they are."

He was right, in a way that made me itch. "You've no idea what I'm afraid of, Hartwell. Now leave me be."

He didn't. Instead, he placed a slip of paper in my palm—folded, plain, and without preamble. "If you want to know why the bodies are showing up like warnings, meet me at the Hare and Hounds. I'm there every evening until half midnight. There are people who'll talk to you, but not to the police. Not even to Roth's men."

I glared at him, wondering where he'd gotten his information. "Are *you* working for the Hammer?"

He barked a laugh. "Christ, no. But sometimes the best way to understand a problem is to see how the syndicates try to solve it."

I made no move to pocket the paper, but he seemed pleased all the same. "You'll want to keep your wits about you," he said, voice once again dropping. "There's a man here —a holy man. He's not who he says he is."

"People rarely are," I quipped, expressing more bitterness than intended.

That stopped him, but only long enough to reset his tactics. He switched from investigative assault to confidential whisper, leaning in as if to share a secret. "I've heard a rumor you're working for Jorah Roth and the Syndicate, but I don't buy it. No disrespect, but you don't have the look of a Company woman. But then again, if you're traveling with the Blade..." He let his smug insinuation drift off into the mist.

I said nothing. If there was one thing every self-respecting Irish girl learned, it was how to make a silence work for you. It wasn't a skill that came naturally, as I'd like to sink my teeth into his throat, but I was learning as I practiced.

Hartwell, however, took it as an invitation to perform. "I think you're here to do what the police can't. And I respect that, honestly. But I'd be careful—very careful—about which side of this story you let yourself be on. There are lines in the country that don't exist in the city."

I let the silence curdle between us, my expression just as sour.

Hartwell's lips twitched, the kind of smile that precedes a punch or a proposition. "You can ignore me, Miss Mahoney, but I'm not leaving. Not until I have the truth—or at least what passes for it in these parts. Off the record, I'd advise you to pick your confidantes carefully. It's not just the police who want answers."

I regarded him, and for the briefest moment, every muscle in his face tensed, betraying the fear that ran beneath his practiced bravado. "If you follow me again, Mr. Hartwell, do yourself the favor of sending for an undertaker first. I'm not a woman who begs a headline."

He cocked his head, feigning hurt. "That's demonstrably false. You're the most interesting woman to come out of Whitechapel since the Canonical Five." He leaned in, his voice softening. "And I know you were Mary Kelly's best mate."

A cold, surgical hush cut through my thoughts. As it did when Mary's name spilled from the lips of men who should have known better.

He waited, savoring the effect, but I made no reply. Only let the silence open and swallow his cleverness. There are few expressions more satisfying than the one a man wears when he realizes he has misjudged the depth of the water he's waded into.

"If you value your tongue," I said after a fraught minute, "you'd do well to keep it from wagging over the bones of the dead. Especially not hers."

Hartwell grinned, but it trembled at the corners. "I meant no disrespect. In fact, I'd argue we're on the same side. The city needs someone who can see past the official version. I only want—"

"Truth?" I cut him off, my voice as thin and clean as piano wire. "Then find it elsewhere. I've survived worse than a byline, Mr. Hartwell, and I'm not above adding another name to London's list of missing persons."

He actually laughed, but it was an ugly, hollow sound. "You'll forgive me if I say I don't entirely believe you. You were always softer than the stories make out. At least, that's what Aberline and Croft say about you when asked. In fact, most of Scotland Yard say they'd never met someone as stalwart as you when it came to bringing justice for a drunken prostitute."

I did not move. I did not breathe. But I felt, all at once, the ghost of her—her laughter in some far-off gin dive and her hand on my wrist, saying, "Don't let them see how you bleed, Fi, but make 'em pay for every drop."

Mary.

She was so much more than a drunken prostitute to me.

Hartwell caught the flicker in my eyes, and for a moment, he seemed almost contrite. But the sort of man who fed on sorrow always mistook it for an invitation, never understanding that some women only raged so they wouldn't drown the world in the salt of their tears.

He tried for a gentler note. "Look, I know what it's like to lose someone to the city's appetite. I'm not trying to exploit you, Miss Mahoney. Really. But the people up the hill—those families—they eat their own, and they'll do the same to you if you let them. I only want to—"

I snapped the case in my hands shut, hard enough to make him step back. "You're dangerously assuming I give a rain-soaked fuck what you want," I bit at him, using the foul language as an evocation of how far I was willing to go for

Mary. "I imagine you don't want to be easily recognized by the Blade, especially if you're asking reckless questions."

I wasn't someone who enjoyed threatening people, as a rule, but I had to say his teeth made the most delightful sound when his mouth clamped shut. Hartwell tipped his hat, and for a brief instant, I caught the glint of real warning in his eyes.

Anger.

Then he vanished down the platform, swallowed by the rain and the crowd of departing passengers.

Only after he'd gone did I realize my hands were shaking. Not from cold, but from the unsettling certainty that, despite all my best efforts, the ghosts of London were still two steps ahead of me.

Night Horse and Celeste re-emerged from the station office. She was in high dudgeon, but even from a distance, I could see she had resolved the issue to her satisfaction. Night Horse's face was unchanged, but his eyes flicked to me, assessing, as if he could smell the disturbance.

I took a steadying breath, wiped the moisture from my spectacles, and readied myself for the next stage of the performance. I knew, with the intimacy of a long-acquainted patient and her disease, that nothing about this visit to Witcombe Green would be tidy.

But at least I had a sense now of the actors on the stage.

And, for the first time in years, I found myself wishing that Jack the Ripper was here to see the spectacle.

At least he'd have appreciated the artistry.

Chapter Five

I f London was a crucible, Witcombe Green was the slag that bubbled to the top: rich, remote, and utterly convinced of its own refinement.

The private carriage deposited us at the foot of an estate so aggressively landscaped that even the starlings seemed to obey its geometry. The drive ran a quarter mile through avenues of imported beech before emptying onto a sweep of gravel so bright in the post-storm sunlight that I half-expected to go snow-blind.

I might have hurt my neck trying to count gables on a mansion that was a monument to Victorian overcompensation.

We'd have been noticed if not for the festival First Night in full swing despite the aftermath of a summer cloud burst.

Banners in garish red and gold rippled from the columns, and the garden had been overrun by a menagerie of tents, each boasting its own peculiar delicacy or diversion. String quartets did battle with a lone piper; sloe gin and claret flowed from casks the size of coffins for the work-a-day revelers. Clusters of children lobbed scones at each other with the aim and malice of artillery officers.

A half-dozen such carriages waited in the circular drive to be offloaded by a regiment of footmen in lavish livery, and it was a good ten minutes before the door opened and a white gloved hand extended.

The air was damp with pollen and the promise of wealth. If I squinted, I could almost ignore the taste of threat that drifted just beneath the surface, sharp as a razor under a kid glove.

Celeste stepped out first, and I saw her as the world did: radiant, unsinkable, a comet of silk and laughter whose wake bent the attention of everyone from the lowest footman to the grand dames themselves. I followed at the appropriate two-step remove, clutching a carpetbag and doing my best imitation of a woman who had never once hidden a blade in her hemline or handled organs with her bare hands.

Night Horse, for his part, vanished the moment the cab door clicked shut, as if he'd melted into the ornamental yews.

Celeste and I ascended the steps in unison, where an imposing servant waited to take our names, bowing with a precision that suggested he could list every hereditary disorder in the family line of his employer, should the need arise.

"Celeste Beaumont, daughter of Madame la Comtesse de St. Germain..." She flicked her fingers at me. "...and party. We are expected by Mrs. Goldsmid."

The servant bowed again, deeper, and ushered us through a hall so luminous with gaslight and gilding that it seemed less a room than a phantasmagoria staged for the benefit of visiting royalty. I lost count of the mirrors, but not the faces —every guest reflected, repeated, made more beautiful or grotesque by the lens of money and the absence of empathy.

We were led past the main ballroom, already thick with

the perfume of anticipation and port, into a smaller salon that managed to be both intimate and ostentatious all at once. The ceiling soared, frescoed with something that looked suspiciously like the martyrdom of a minor saint. The furniture was arranged in conversational clusters, each one a microcosm of power: here, a trio of judges and their wives, each more severe than the last; there, a clutch of foreign diplomats, circled like wolves around a platter of smoked fish. In the far corner, a very old woman in widow's black presided over a younger, jumpier cohort, her gaze so sharp she seemed to be counting the molecules of oxygen between words.

It was the kind of room that made you feel both invisible and observed, and I could already tell which was the safer option.

"Ah, my darling Celeste!" cried a voice from the gallery above. A woman in violet silk and a tiara made of honest-to-God sapphires swept down the stairs, arms open.

"Mrs. Goldsmid," Celeste greeted warmly.

Our hostess was the sort of beauty that persisted well after youth had fled—her figure still imposing, her hair an uncompromising white, her eyes the flinty blue of glacial lakes. She clasped Celeste's hands, then pressed a kiss to both cheeks, French-style.

"You grow more luminous with each year," Mrs. Goldsmid declared. "And this—" She turned to me with a gaze that assessed every seam of my dress, every freckle on my skin, every millimeter of my waist. "—is your companion?"

Celeste's tone shifted, demure and businesslike. "Miss Mahoney, my indispensable right hand. She manages my correspondence, schedules, and all else besides. She is also—" here Celeste allowed a sly smile. "—a woman of particular intellect and interests."

This seemed to amuse Lady Goldsmid immensely.

"A pleasure, madam," I said, keeping my accent just on the

Irish side of neutral, enough to mark me as Outsider but not enough to invite comment.

A chime sounded, and the company began drifting toward the garden, drawn by the prospect of food, festival, or gossip. Lady Goldsmid led the way, arm-in-arm with Celeste, leaving me to follow in their wake.

Having been conscripted into a detective's position I was woefully under prepared for, I tried cataloging everything for possible future analysis.

The way the judges' wives whispered behind their fans.

The way the old woman in black flicked her eyes from face to face, like an auditor tallying souls.

The way one of the Russian guests—tall, blond, perfectly blank—kept his gaze fixed not on the party, but on the doors, as if awaiting an invasion or a message.

Outside, the tented pavilion was a study in cheerful excess. Tablecloths in vermillion and gold, chandeliers strung like captured stars, platters of sweets and smoked fish and canapés so delicate they dissolved on the tongue. I poured myself a cup of summer rum punch and sipped, careful to keep my hands steady. You could always spot the nervous ones by the way they overindulged in the first hour of a party.

Celeste was already working the crowd, threading her way through knots of aristocrats and merchants, flashing her smile like a lantern. She knew how to light a room, and more importantly, how to keep herself in the penumbra just adjacent to power. I watched her circulate—one moment bright laughter with a dowager in peacock green, the next an intimate, whispered aside to a sandy-mustached baronet, who nearly spilled his drink in the effort to catch every word. Within five minutes, she'd mapped the grounds, set the currents running in her favor, and established that she was both desirable and above reproach.

I trailed after, playing the part of the discreetly attentive assistant. This meant I was mostly invisible, except to the other ghosts who haunted the servant's stations: the under-butlers, the footmen, and the occasional governess or companion peer with more wits than prospects. We were a race apart, free to overhear everything because no one truly cared we existed.

It was hard to express the juxtaposition of relief and offense.

A sudden hush overtook the revelers, followed closely by a whispering din.

Someone important had arrived.

All eyes turned to the drive where a remarkable carriage might as well have been dispensing royalty.

The first to appear was Count Leonid Ivanovich Vronsky, a tall, slim fellow who cut a severe figure in a black tailcoat and white gloves. He moved with the slightly bow-legged gait of a cavalry officer, and his silver beard was trimmed to the strictest regulation.

His wife, Lady Vronskya, wore a collar of rubies so thick it looked like a sparkling wound, and her smile didn't quite reach her eyes.

Their son—Alexei—looked as if he'd been carved from the same pale wood as the trees lining the estate: blond, tall, and too beautiful for his own good. He moved with the restless energy of a predator confined to a petting zoo, scanning the crowd for challenge or entertainment.

"Celeste! Darling!" he called upon spotting her, his voice ringing clear across the lawn. She turned, radiating delight, and let him kiss her hand in the Continental style. They fell instantly into a rapid, bantering French, forgetting my existence completely.

The couple was so exceedingly handsome, they drew every eye.

As I shadowed Celeste through her social rounds, I

caught snippets of the underlying gossip: talk of the recent exhumations, speculation on who would be next, and a thread of nastier rumor about the nature of the Vronskys, the rising civil unrest in Russia and their attachment to it.

It was said they'd made their money in something so scandalous that even the Russians pretended not to know. I heard opium, then arms dealing, then a black market in holy relics. It was also said the family's ties to the Romanovs were both literal and bloody—that somewhere in the house was a painting that had been stabbed and sewn back together, because the original subject had displeased the Tsar.

I made a mental note to ask Celeste if she'd ever seen it.

At the edge of the lawn, in the shade of a copper beech, a group of guests clustered around an elderly rabbi and a young, well-dressed man. The rabbi was hunched, his beard yellowed from pipe smoke. He gesticulated with his stick, arguing some fine point.

"We cannot wait for the coroner," the old man declared. "It is not fitting. The soul cannot rest unless the body is whole, and the tradition is very clear: burial must occur before sunset of the second day."

A younger, more cynical voice cut in. "But what if the death was not natural? How do we explain to the authorities that we have hurried the body into the ground, and then expect justice for what happened? There are already whispers that we hide something."

The rabbi spat on the grass. "Whispers! There will always be whispers, but a Jew who breaks the burial law is no better than a goy. If the English police want their inspection, let them have the corpse now, before the Sabbath."

A matron in heavy black, who looked as though she'd buried three husbands by teatime, intervened. "What is it you expect to find? If the body was murdered, it is an insult; if it was not, it is an abomination to open the grave again. There is no dignity in this either way."

"That is precisely the point," said the young man, shifting his weight. "If someone is sending a message, we must understand the message. These—these exhumations are not mere vandalism. They are statements. And the statements will not stop until someone reads them correctly."

I drifted closer, adopting the posture of a disinterested staff, eyes fixed on the hedge while my ears strained for every word.

The rabbi turned to the banker, eyes glittering. "And what message do you suppose is being sent, Mr. Pinski?"

Pinski made a derisive sound. "If I knew, I would say...but I assume it's a message not written for a Brit."

A ripple of tension, then the rabbi leaned in. "You think it is a vendetta? An old-world blood feud?"

"I think it is about money," the banker replied. "It is always about money, or the lack thereof."

The rabbi snorted. "Your faith is small, Mr. Pinski. Money is only one of the evils that evoke such crimes."

"And your faith is a luxury," said the banker, "when the rent on these houses grows higher every year."

The conversation dissolved as a pageboy announced lunch, and the group dispersed, still muttering.

I made a note: the conflict was not just about tradition versus law, but about survival in the unspoken economy of the immigrant elite. Every person in this garden knew their standing could be erased by a single scandal—and the consequences thereof would be felt by the entire community seeking a new home on Albion.

Inside, the lunch was a staged opera of civility. The table sat forty and every place card was a chess move. Celeste was bracketed by Alexei and a scion of the Guinness fortune, while I was placed near the foot, among elevated staff such as governesses, elderly aunts-turned-chaperones, and the local clergy.

Night Horse was nowhere to be seen, which sparked an anger in my breast on his behalf.

Surely he'd despise the rules of this table, but the reason the invitation was likely not extended stuck like a thorn in my heart.

His skin and style wouldn't have matched ours.

The conversation at my end was muted, something forgettable about the difficulties of importing French wine after the latest tariff. I kept my attention on the head of the table, where Lady Goldsmid and Lady Vronskya took turns directing the flow, and Celeste held court from the middle. The topics ranged from art (a new Klimt acquired in Vienna) to politics (the Home Secretary's alleged mistress) to the "tragic events of recent weeks," which were discussed in the vague, polite terms reserved for fainting fits and house fires.

But beneath the froth, I felt the undertow: the real subject was fear. Every guest, from the highest to the lowest, was watching for the next sign that their carefully maintained world might be coming apart.

When I sat in a room such as this, I felt out of my depth. Every single glittering reveler appeared to be holding their breath over a lie, and I knew so little about them I'd not even begun to speculate what those were. How did Jorah expect me to solve this? The three previous times I'd uncovered a killer, I'd done so because of something I'd found or overheard at a murder scene.

I'd not gone looking for a mystery, I'd been pulled into it kicking and screaming.

After the third course, a footman delivered a note to my place. It was a single line, in Celeste's script: "Library. Fifteen minutes."

I excused myself, made the rounds of the corridor with

due care, and slipped into the library, which was, of course, bigger than my entire rowhouse back home. The air inside was cool and damp, the light filtered through burgundy drapes. I didn't know who I expected to find, but Night Horse stood by the window, examining a book with a look of genuine interest.

He didn't turn when I entered. "You made a friend of the rabbi," he said, voice low.

"I try to blend," I replied. "Did you find what you needed?"

He shut the book, replaced it with surgical precision. "We need to see the body before they bury it."

"How do we get into the morgue?" I asked.

Only his eyes smiled down at me. "Meet me there at eleven, I'll get us in."

I nodded. "I'll bring my kit."

He paused, gazing down at me, his features hidden in shadows. "Be careful," he finally said.

I wanted to ask what he'd been doing in Paris, why he'd left me to face my nightmares alone, but it would have been a waste of breath.

Instead, I let the silence fill my heart and returned to the table, preparing to spend the dark hours in his company.

Chapter Six

B reaking into a morgue was a new transgression, even for me.

The darkness of Witcombe Green clung like a second skin as we approached the ivy-covered brick building that abutted the overgrown cemetery.

Here we were, Night Horse and I, two unwanted foreign stains on the pristine fabric of the English countryside, doing the devil's handiwork while the locals danced and drank the night away.

No moon dared show its face tonight—a blessing for our illicit venture, though my racing heart seemed loud enough to wake the dead we'd come to visit. The crisp summer night air nipped at my cheeks, but beneath my bodice, sweat gathered between my shoulder blades.

"Are you certain this is necessary?" I whispered, my breath forming ghostly plumes in the frigid air. "If the corpse was five days dead and the autopsy performed, what would we find that the coroner hasn't already?"

Night Horse didn't answer immediately. His silence was as much a part of him as his long black hair or the scars that mapped his hands like constellations. When he finally spoke, his voice was low, measured, each word selected with the precision of a surgeon choosing a scalpel. "Their Coroner is the country doctor recruited to sign paperwork," he muttered. "No more scientist than a tonic peddler."

"I see." I wrinkled my nose and yearned for Dr. Phillips, the coroner I'd met during Mary Kelly's murder inquest. He was a thorough scientist and a precise surgeon—a luxury of which the pastoral murder victim could hardly ever take advantage.

"The dead have secrets they cannot hide from those who know how to listen." I felt more than saw Night Horse's dark gaze find me, and the sensation was both chilling and thrilling at once. "You are the only other person I know who can hear."

I swallowed hard, knowing he meant it as a compliment. "Let's just hope no one else is trying to listen to Mr. Auerbach tonight." My attempt at levity fell heavily to the gravel.

"Stay low," Night Horse murmured, crouching at the edge of the shadowed rock wall.

We crept around the squat stone building, its windows dark, save for a single flickering light near the entrance. The night attendant's post. The Witcombe Green morgue had once been a chapel, before progress and death had claimed it for more practical purposes. The irony wasn't lost on me; one house of eternal rest converted to another.

Night Horse guided me around to a side entrance, his hand at the small of my back, neither pushing nor pulling— merely present, like gravity. He moved with a predator's grace, feet barely disturbing the gravel beneath us. I tried to match his steps, feeling clumsy and loud by comparison.

The side yard was a field of crusted mud and half-drowned dahlias, each flower pockmarked and sagging like the face of a long-suffering parishioner. Overhead, a single gas lamp flickered, doing its best to keep the darkness from groping too far.

The night attendant's snores reached us before we saw him—a rhythmic, wet sound like a handsaw through damp wood. I peered around the corner to find him slumped in his chair, mouth agape, a half-empty bottle of gin providing explanation enough for his deep slumber. A tattered penny dreadful lay open on his lap, its lurid cover depicting a swooning woman and a dark figure wielding a knife.

How fitting.

"The keys," Night Horse murmured close to my ear, his breath warm against my cold skin.

With a startle of movement against my thigh, Night Horse removed a set of keys from the pocket of his coat.

"Where did you get those?" I asked, aghast.

"From his pocket two hours ago at the festival." He wiggled his deft, skilled fingers at me and I had to duck my head to hide a blush.

There were times I wondered how Night Horse had survived all the violence of his past...

And there were other times I wondered how anyone else had.

The lock yielded with a reluctant groan that made my teeth clench. We froze, watching the attendant, but his snores continued uninterrupted.

Night Horse pushed the door open just wide enough for us to slip through, then closed it behind us with a practiced lack of sound.

Inside, the morgue embraced us with its chill—a cold different from the damp evening air outside.

The chill of absence, of life departed.

The smell hit me next, that distinctive blend of chemical preservation and organic decay that no amount of cleaning could ever fully banish. I'd smelled it countless times in my work as a Post-Mortem Sanitation Specialist, yet it always made something primitive in my brain prepare for danger.

We carefully muffled our footsteps on stone floors stained the color of old tea. Decades of spilled formaldehyde, bodily fluids, and God knew what else had left their mark, telling stories I could read as clearly as others read books.

A particularly dark patch near the doorway spoke of a hemorrhage case from years past; a splash pattern along the baseboards whispered of a dissection gone messily awry.

This morgue wasn't well kept or well run.

"This way," I said, taking the lead. I'd been in enough morgues to navigate their general layout.

The gaslights had been turned low for the night, casting elongated shadows that danced across the walls as we moved. Our own silhouettes stretched before us like harbingers from the netherworld.

Night Horse's footfalls were barely perceptible behind me, but I could feel his presence like a physical weight. He carried with him an intensity that charged the air, making the fine hairs on my arms stand at attention despite the chill. I glanced back once to find his dark eyes scanning our surroundings, alert for any threat. His hand hovered near his hip, where I knew he kept one of his many blades.

We reached a battered door marked 'STORAGE.' The black letters were stenciled in a tremulous hand that must have belonged to someone with a sense of humor or a profound lack of self-preservation. I tried the handle and found it unlatched; the cold that rushed out was sharp enough to make my teeth ache, and the darkness inside pressed outward, as if held back by nothing more than indifference.

We stepped into the black, shutting the door with a snick that sounded, in the hush, like a pistol shot. A quick fumble found the wall sconce. The feeble gaslight flared and hissed, leaking illumination down thin limestone steps.

"The attendant didn't seem close to rousing," I assured him, though whether I was trying to convince him or myself remained unclear.

"It's not him I'm concerned about," Night Horse replied, his gaze meeting mine briefly before descending the stairs ahead of me.

The implication hung between us, unspoken but understood. Someone had murdered Jacob Auerbach—someone who might not appreciate our amateur investigation.

The foot of the stairwell opened into a large, cold stone cellar. Two examination tables dominated the room, only one of them in use. A sheet-draped form rested motionless on a slab of ice, beneath the flickering gaslight overhead that cast eerie, dancing shadows across the white linen. As the ice melted, it dripped noisily onto the floor before running into the drain.

"My people would find your people's treatment of the dead something out of a horror tale," Night Horse said, lifting his lip in a silent snarl at the tableau.

"What do your people do with their dead?" I asked gently.

"Instead of moving the departed, we moved the village," he stated simply, inspecting a bone saw with skilled interest.

I paused, so many questions occurring to me I picked the silliest one. "How do you mark the grave?"

He leveled me a challenging look. "We would leave the dead beneath the sky so they could find their way to the—you'd call it heaven."

My mouth dropped open. "You just leave it there? Wouldn't scavengers get to it?"

"Yes." He looked at me askance, shrugging his wide shoulders. "But that is the way it should be. Animals die so we may eat them. When we die, they may eat us."

"But...But..." I tried very hard not to think of a wolf with a human bone in his mouth, tugging on it like my neighbor's hounds.

His features relaxed at my distress. "To bury the dead would mean to trap their spirit beneath the ground."

I understood immediately, though the thought processes differed, the deference to the dead remained the same.

I thought of his murdered wife and daughter and a tear burned at the corner of my eye. "Our country must be very sad for you then...We bury all our dead. You believe them all trapped ghosts?"

A darkness slid over his expression. "No. I don't believe in gods or ghosts. Yours or mine."

I wasn't certain what to say then, so I nodded my ascent and turned back to the issue at hand.

Cabinets and shelves lined the walls, holding instruments whose purpose I could only partially guess at, though Dr. Phillips had educated me on many during our professional interactions.

My steps faltered as I neared the table. Despite my profession and all I'd seen, there remained something deeply transgressive about what we were doing. Jacob Auerbach had been buried according to Jewish custom, then exhumed by someone with no respect for his state of being...

Or, rather, not being.

And now here we were, disturbing his rest yet again.

"Forgive me," I whispered, not sure if I was addressing Auerbach or the God who'd abandoned me years ago.

My hands trembled slightly as I reached for the sheet. The fabric felt rough and cold beneath my fingers, slightly damp from the room's chill. I peeled it back, slow and careful, as if the corpse might object.

Jacob Auerbach stared up at me with the resigned expression of a man who'd outlived all his creditors. His lips were drawn back in a rictus grin, and the tip of his nose had turned an improbable shade of decay.

Death did not flatter him, but I'd seen worse. If God blessed me at all, it was that someone had put him on a thick slab of ice to prevent even more rot than had already occurred.

I'd learned long ago that bodies spoke their own language. Dr. Phillips had been my reluctant tutor in this morbid tongue, his precise hands guiding mine over the geography of death until I could read the stories written in bruised flesh and stiffened limbs. Auerbach's body had plenty to say, despite someone's hasty efforts to silence it.

The burial had been performed with speed, and now I understood why.

Someone had been desperate to hide the true violence of his end.

"He's been embalmed," Night Horse noted with surprise. "I know from Roth that it is not the practice of Jews to embalm their dead. They are to bury before sun sets on the next day and return to dust."

"And thank God for that. Neither of us would survive in this room had he been putrefying for this long. The smell is bad enough as it is." I gulped against the scent of death and extracted some lavender oil from my bag to rub beneath my nose.

The embalming was worth noting since it wasn't common practice. Another issue with the local coroner? or something more sinister?

If he was murdered, why would someone want to preserve the evidence of that, and then dig up the body when they'd gotten away with it?

"They've cleaned him," I murmured, leaning closer to examine the pale skin. "But not well enough."

Night Horse moved back to the foot of the stairs to stand sentinel against the door. "What do you see?"

I lit the lamp and pulled it closer, adjusting it to cast better illumination across Auerbach's torso. "Lacerations. Someone tried to wash them clean, but there's still evidence." I ran a gloved finger along a thin, nearly invisible line across the abdomen.

No need to stitch a corpse that would be buried before anyone could look too closely.

"Three primary wounds," I noted, falling into the clinical pattern I'd adopted from Dr. Phillips. "Left to right across the abdomen, with the final one penetrating the lungs. But these smaller incisions..." I traced the air above a pattern of tiny, almost delicate cuts low on his belly. "These were made after death. See how the skin has reacted differently?" A puckered incision that had been patched up by someone in a visible hurry had never leaked blood to begin with.

So why stitch it?

Night Horse stepped closer, his curiosity briefly overcoming his vigilance. "Whoever did it wanted something from him," he said.

"Or wanted something in him," I replied.

I reached for the scissors in my kit and snipped the thread, careful not to mar the skin beneath. The cut opened with a wet sigh. There was no blood, of course, only the syrupy remains of what had been pumped in to replace it. I expected to find the usual, but what I extracted from the cut with long-nosed tweezers slipped out of my grip almost immediately.

I knelt, my skirts pooling around me on the filthy floor. A small, folded fragment lay there, no larger than a calling card. With careful fingers, I retrieved it, noting the texture—not paper, but parchment—the kind used for important documents or...

"Religious texts," I breathed, unfolding it with trembling hands. I cleared my throat. "*Et iterum venturus est cum gloria...*' He shall come again with glory."

"You read the Hebrew language?" Night Horse asked, and I hated to dispel the impressed note in his voice.

"This isn't Hebrew, I'm afraid," I muttered. "It's Latin."

I didn't know Latin...but I knew the religion of my Irish family and the idioms the church made us memorize in school.

Night Horse frowned. "Catholic, then?"

"Too Catholic," I said, setting the note aside. "Why would a Jewish banker die with a Catholic prophecy in his gut?"

"Like a ritual," Night Horse observed, his voice so quiet it barely disturbed the air.

The word sent a chill through me that had nothing to do with the morgue's temperature. "Yes," I agreed, the pieces beginning to align in my mind. "Exactly like a ritual."

The implications settled over us like a shroud. "Someone wanted to send a message. Or perhaps..." I hesitated, the thought almost too terrible to voice. "Perhaps it was part of the ritual itself and only God was supposed to read it."

"Catholics and Jews share the same God," Night Horse remembered out loud. "But take different paths of blood to him."

I recalled the bodies I'd cleaned over the years—the foreign or disenfranchised victims of violence whose deaths were often dismissed by authorities as unfortunate but not worth thorough investigation. Auerbach had been different only in his wealth and standing. Someone had gone to great lengths to hide the true nature of his death, arranging a quick burial before questions could be asked.

"There's a partial monogram on the back." Night Horse turned the unfolded paper over where a red monogram had been stamped and torn, less than a quarter of it visible. "This isn't red ink."

I looked closer, and my stomach turned. He was right. The deep umber of the symbol didn't appear to be ink at all, but blood.

"Sweet Mary," I whispered, invoking a deity I wasn't sure I still believed in.

With careful movements, I extracted a clean handkerchief from my pocket and wrapped the parchment fragment in its folds. The evidence was light as a feather, but it felt heavy as I tucked it away, weighted with implications that reached far beyond murder.

"This isn't just about grave robbery or a personal vendetta against Auerbach or the others. The Christian symbolism on a Jewish corpse..." I met Night Horse's steady gaze. "This has the stink of something older. Something biblical."

"Religious hatred," he agreed, his voice flat. "It never truly dies, just finds new vessels."

I nodded, thinking of the hundreds of years of sectarian war against my own people. The Jewish community had faced increasing hostility in recent years, with whispered accusations and age-old prejudices finding fertile ground in economic uncertainty. But this—this suggested organization, purpose. Perhaps even ecclesiastical involvement.

It was an escalation that could have national consequences.

"We need to know who that monogram belongs to," I said, standing and pulling the sheet back over Auerbach's violated body. The simple act felt like both apology and promise. "And we need to find out who ordered or conducted his exhumation, and why."

There was a clatter from the hall. Night Horse's hand went to his waistcoat, where he kept a weapon I'd not seen yet but was confident existed. I snuffed the lamp and ducked behind the table, the corpse an unwilling accomplice in our game of hide-and-seek. Night Horse melted into the shadows, only the whites of his eyes betraying his position.

A minute passed, maybe less. The sound resolved into the shambling gait of the attendant, who entered the room with a lantern held high and a bottle of gin clutched low. He scuffled down the short stairs, gave the corpse a once-over, checked the lock on the cabinet, and shuffled out, never noticing the two living souls breathing mere arm's length away.

I let out the breath I'd been holding and stood, brushing brick dust from my sleeves. Night Horse relaxed his stance but did not entirely lose the edge.

"We're done here," he said.

I looked at Jacob Auerbach. "I think he's told us all he can."

Night Horse nodded once, then gestured toward the door. "We've been here too long."

He was right. We'd tempted fate enough for one night. As I cast one final glance at Auerbach's shrouded form, I felt the weight of the parchment in my pocket—a fragment of evidence that connected a Jewish financier's death to Christian ritual. My heart pounded against my ribs as the realization solidified: the conspiracy reached far beyond simple grave robbery or a vendetta born of Shenanigans. Something darker lurked beneath Witcombe Green's idyllic landscape, something that had centuries of hatred feeding its hunger.

All I could do was keep digging and hope I didn't end up on the slab beside him.

Chapter Seven

✦

I f the wealthy loved anything, it was a late dinner with as many courses as possible.

The following night found me exhausted from trailing Celeste around the hot, humid festival all afternoon. Now, having changed into one of two silk dinner gowns, I stifled the loud growl of my stomach as we approached the most exclusive table in the county.

The Goldsmid estate's dining hall was a cathedral to English opulence. The effect on the retinas was somewhere between an epileptic fit and a religious vision.

The only thing more cutting than the crystal was the conviction I did not belong.

I trailed two paces behind Celeste and might as well have been wrapped in sackcloth and ashes rather than violet and black lace for all the attention my presence drew. Or so I thought, until the butler announced our arrival and every face at the table pivoted in unison, a parade of marbled gazes sizing me up with the speculative interest usually reserved for sideshow oddities.

"The Right Honorable Miss Beaumont and her esteemed

companion, Miss Mahoney," the butler intoned, with just enough hesitation on "companion" to suggest a world of unsavory possibilities.

The orchestrated seating plan had the precision of a masterful military maneuver, positioning each dinner guest with strategic intent.

Celeste was strategically placed next to the notorious Alexei Vronsky, whose broad-shouldered handsomeness and sly smile seemed straight out of a scandalous novel. He seemed to embody the very spirit of those reckless-yet-gallant heroes that mothers warned their daughters about, and the glint in his eye was nothing short of conspiratorial and charming.

Meanwhile, my own position at the elongated mahogany table felt like an afterthought, as if I were a footnote at an otherwise significant event. I was relegated to the far end amongst assorted clergymen and a collection of spinster aunts with my same supposed position in life.

To my left sat Reverend Blackwood, his presence colder than a graveyard breeze on a moonless night. His visage seemed perpetually ensconced in shadow, even beneath the brilliant glow of chandeliers. Across from him, with an expression as kindly as it was wise, sat the rabbi from the festival—a figure of warmth and wisdom who wore spectacles strikingly akin to my own. His beard was an impressive monument to patience and tradition as were tidy curls at his ear.

The Anglican vicar some two spaces down completed our improbable trio of holy men. He was a rotund gentleman whose florid complexion betrayed both his affection for rich foods and his discomfort in such opulent surroundings. He'd sweated through his first handkerchief before the second course arrived.

He was not a man whose heart or liver were long for this world.

The opening volley of conversation was as boring as you'd suspect, all pleasantries and platitudes. Once the third course of five was served, rhetoric had devolved to a contest to see which guest could subtly reference the recent immigrant unrest in London while maintaining plausible deniability.

Reverend Blackwood was an early favorite, sliding into the topic with the subtlety of a guillotine. "I find it heartening, that even in these troubled times, men of faith can break bread together. It's a testament to the endurance of traditional Christian English values."

A visible tic pulsed in the rabbi's jaw, but he returned serve with a patient smile. "London is a city of many traditions, Reverend. We find strength in our diversity."

Blackwood's lips twitched, as if a more honest reply had tried to stage a coup but was suppressed at the last instant. "Yes, well, let's hope that strength is not tested too severely. I worry for the young, myself." His gaze flicked to Alexei, then to Celeste, and then—deliberately—to me. "They're so easily led astray."

I could almost hear the vicar's sphincter clench in sympathetic embarrassment. He launched a doomed rescue attempt. "I find this upcoming generation to be most invigorating, Father Blackwood," the jowly vicar murmured. "They're much kinder and more likely to provide charity to the needy and finance the progress of medicine and science, which brings us more blessings and knowledge from heaven."

Blackwood sneered, not to be denied his kill. "Of course, it's our *Christian* duty to care for the poor and the displaced, but these bleeding-heart youths obsessed with pleasure and progress must be careful. Charity breeds dependence, and dependence breeds resentment. Eventually, the wolf you feed grows hungry for shepherd's blood."

The line hung over the table, as bitter as the soup.

Celeste, ever the diplomat, steered the topic to Parisian fashion, where even Blackwood's fanaticism lost its edge. For a few blessed minutes I could indulge in the spectacle of the upper classes performing their favorite ritual: pretending not to notice that the world was on fire outside the manor walls.

There was safety in these shallow waters, but I'd never learned to float.

I turned my attention to the rabbi, who had spent the last several minutes alternating between polite silence and outright self-defense. We exchanged a look, the universal sign for "Neither of us belong here, shall we be allies?"

"Miss Mahoney, could you share a phrase with us in the native Irish tongue?" the rabbi asked, a hint of curiosity brightening his otherwise weary eyes. "I recently heard Gaelic spoken and found its melody quite enchanting."

I grinned, feeling a mix of nerves and delight. "Well, I can give it a try. There's '*Go n-éirí an bóthar leat, agus go mbuailimid le chéile arís, go gcoinní Dia i mbos a láimhe thú*,' which means 'may the road rise to meet you, and until we meet again may God hold you in the hollow of His hand.'"

The rabbi's eyes sparkled with warmth. "That's lovely. In Hebrew, we say '*b'seter elyon*,' meaning 'under the shadow of the Almighty,' hoping God watches over us."

We both chuckled softly, sharing a moment of cultural exchange and delight. Just then, the reverend interjected with a gentle yet firm tone, "In this country, manners dictate we keep our conversation in English."

The Rabbi offered him a tight-lipped apology, but when the reverend turned to receive mine, I held his gaze for two full and silent sips of my soup.

By the time the main course arrived, the ambient level of tension was high enough to curdle the hollandaise. The vicar had given up all pretense of control, focusing instead on getting as much food into his mouth as possible without drawing attention. Blackwood, not content with dominating the room, began to "accidentally" brush my elbow with his.

He waited until the servants were clearing the second course before striking.

He stood, his glass raised high, commanding the attention of everyone at the table. "In honor of the Goldsmids and the Vronskys," he began, his tone laced with a veneer of respect, "whose contributions are almost as memorable as their presence here tonight. Truly, it takes a special kind of ingenuity to make such an impact." He paused, a sly smile playing on his lips. "And now, let us toast to England and the Queen—*per aspera ad astra.*"

Through suffering to the stars.

My blood chilled, then surged. This phrase wasn't stitched into the parchment found on the dead financier's wound, but it hit me like a blunt ax that a catholic priest would of course be fluent in Latin. I masked my unease with a sip of wine, while my mind raced ahead.

The rest of the table muttered appreciative noises and lifted their glasses. I cataloged Blackwood's tells: the finger drumming, the predatory scan of the room, the way he waited just a fraction of a second too long before returning the rabbi's smile.

For a man of God, he was disturbingly good at the mechanics of subtle intimidation.

If England had a second religion, it was that of after-dinner digestion. The Goldsmids were no exception. No sooner had the servants cleared away the remains of the saccharine final course than the company migrated *en masse* to the drawing room, that purgatory where decency and decorum fought their nightly duel over the remains of sherry and old gossip.

The men clustered by the fireplace, where a sullen coal

fire provided more ambiance than warmth on a summer's evening.

The women—Lady Goldsmid, Vronsky, Celeste, and one or two outliers—arrayed themselves on velvet settees, their conversation a polite hum punctuated by occasional shrieks of laughter at stories that, to my ear, sounded more like deathbed confessions.

I took up a position in the no-man's land between, close enough to eavesdrop, far enough to avoid conscription into either camp. Having grown with more than a handful of brothers, I'd turned eavesdropping into an art before I'd climbed out from behind my ma's apron.

Reverend Blackwood, liberated from the constraints of the dinner table, found a new audience in the form of Lord Vronsky and the lesser sons of England's gentry. They stood at the upstairs parlor window, gazing down on the Second Night festival revelry like Gods from Olympus selecting their enemies and their lovers.

The subject, inevitably, was the "natural order" of things, and how much effort was required to preserve it from the "onslaught of foreign degeneracy." He said this with the air of a man unveiling a new species of orchid, not the cold arithmetic of genocide.

"It's the principle of the matter," Blackwood said, swirling a glass of port as if it contained the answers to all England's ills. "A nation that does not defend its borders—spiritual or otherwise—is doomed to rot from within. Our traditions are what make us great."

Lord Vronsky, in his cups and enjoying the performance, nodded vigorously. "Da, da! In Russia, we shoot them. Very clean. No more problem."

"How very American of them," the rabbi sniffed.

There was a general murmur of approval, the kind that came from men convinced they were being both witty and daring. I could see the rabbi at the edge of the room, isolated in a sea of broadcloth and braying laughter, face set in a mask of rabbinical calm. The vicar, less practiced in the art of public humiliation, had retreated into the bosom of the upholstery, where he was losing a spirited battle with the drowsing effects of claret and rich food.

I made my way to Celeste, who was holding court with Lady Goldsmid. "Your Parisian years must have been so invigorating," cooed Lady Goldsmid. "How does one ever return to our provincial little island?"

"By steamer," Celeste replied, with just enough mischief to register as rebellion. "And by remembering that one's friends are here." She caught my eye and patted the seat beside her. "Come, Fiona. Tell us what plagues the underworld of London these days."

"Scarlet fever and Typhus, mostly," I muttered, and the other women laughed with the relief of people assured that, whatever their faults, at least they would never be that poor.

At one point in my life, I might have aspired to be welcome in such an extravagant room, but the reality was that nothing could be worth this greasy, leaden weight in my guts.

Alexei Vronsky, who had spent the better part of an hour circling the room like a restless shark, suddenly drew everyone's attention by thumping his glass on the sideboard and clearing his throat with a flourish.

"Dear friends," he said, in accented English that was only slightly wounded by vodka, "I have something to say."

He looked at Celeste, then to his mother, then to the entire room.

The silence that followed was almost pure.

"I have known Miss Celeste for over a month," he said, "but I have known from the first moment that she is my—" He searched for the word. "—my destiny."

There was a ripple of amusement, quickly tamped down by Lady Goldsmid's death glare.

"I wish to make official proposal," he said, and with a grandiose motion dropped to one knee before Celeste. From his coat, he produced a velvet box, the kind that telegraphed intentions even to the colorblind. "My dearest Celeste, will you be my wife?" he asked, opening the box to reveal a diamond the size of a newborn's tooth.

I heard Celeste's breath catch. I saw the quick dart of her eyes to Lady Goldsmid, to me, to the rabbi—who alone of the company looked genuinely surprised and delighted.

"Yes," she whispered. "Yes, Alexei, of course I will."

The room erupted. Champagne was summoned, and even the vicar roused himself to offer a felicitation.

In the commotion, I hadn't noticed Reverend Blackwood had slid up beside me. "A lovely event after all the darkness plaguing these grounds of late. I'm surprised the Goldsmids went forward with the festival this year. Someone bobbing for apples is as likely to catch a corpse."

My glare glanced off him as I turned away from the conversation, hoping he'd read the dismissal written into every line of my body.

Disgusting men like him hated to be dismissed. It made them all the more likely to engage.

"Come now," he blustered. "I know who you are, Fiona Mahoney, I read about you in the Times regarding the burning of the tabernacle in Whitechapel...and that business with the multiple murderer, Kathrine Reilly." He rocked back on his heels a little, as if celebrating that he'd uncovered something, though I hadn't especially been trying to hide. "Did you give up on your business of blood, then?" he taunted. "Abandon a grisly trade for a girly one?"

Every word he said made my very skin crawl. "I gave up looking for the ghosts in my past," I lied.

He let out a sound between a scoff and a sigh. "Quite right, it's best to keep one's eyes on the future."

"I prefer the present," I said. "Easier to survive."

"Not for everyone." He studied me, his eyes black as burnt sugar, then melted back into the crowd as I contemplated whether he'd meant that as a threat.

The engagement party proper began, and the Goldsmid estate transformed from a powder keg to a bacchanal.

I watched the Goldsmids congratulate themselves on another successful merger, watched Celeste accept kisses and well-wishes from people who would not remember her name if she and Alexei settled in France, a country kinder to their Russian immigrants. I watched Alexei beam, a man intoxicated by the sudden certainty of his future.

But mostly, I watched Blackwood, who never once lost sight of me. Not even when the music started, not even when the rabbi quietly excused himself and left the room, shoulders stiff and back straight.

I stood at the edge of the revelry, glass of champagne untouched, mind running like a rat through the back alleys of London.

Above the din, I heard Blackwood's voice, reciting some platitude about love and destiny and the will of God.

I wanted to laugh, but all I could think of was the corpse in the morgue, its secrets sewn into the fabric of the night. The world was full of predators, and most of them never even bothered to hide their teeth.

But those who could...the wolves who convinced the sheep they were the shepherd?

Life had taught me they were the most dangerous beasts.

Chapter Eight

✦

The sign above the Hare and Hounds tavern was as subtle as a blow to the head: a painted tableau of two animals locked in toothy embrace, eyes glinting with shared cunning and mutual loathing. It was not the sort of place one went for enlightenment, unless enlightenment came in the form of a cracked mug and a fresh bruise. I told myself I was only there for the ambience, but the truth was—as usual—I was chasing a ghost at midnight, this time in the person of Daniel Hartwell.

I found him at a back table, already two pints in and feigning disappointment that I'd arrived on time. The Hare and Hound was empty except for a few locals whose loyalty to local yeast exceeded any fealty to the festival. Their voices spooled out in low, continuous murmurs, weaving a kind of crude privacy curtain around our corner table. Daniel slid a whisky across the worn wood with a practiced flick.

"I brought no notebook. Swear it," he said, raising both hands as if preparing to be frisked.

"Don't insult me, Hartwell," I muttered. "You'll write your story on your own bones if you have to."

He grinned, not at all offended, and cradled his glass. "To new beginnings."

And, perhaps, to the dead who never quite stayed buried.

I traced the rim of my tumbler and let the silence sprawl a little, savoring the warmth that only good whisky and a total lack of pretense could produce. Outside, a wind was picking up, and I could hear the brush of branches against the window like someone scrawling messages in code.

"You're not at all what I expected, Miss Mahoney," Daniel said, eyes half-lidded and sleepy looking, though his mind was working overtime. "I read all about the Whitechapel case. You're supposed to be haunted. Yet here you sit, perfectly at peace."

I tilted my head. "That's what being haunted means, Hartwell. You grow accustomed to the ghosts."

He laughed at that, the sound bright and sharp. "You and I have more than most, Mahoney." He lifted his glass and drank lustily.

"Before you start," I said, "we set ground rules. Nothing I say leaves this table, not unless I tell you otherwise. And if you try to quote me, I'll make sure your editor is reconstructing your bones."

Hartwell gave a small, tight smile. "Off the record. I understand. I'm not the Met."

"You're worse," I said. "They only hang you if you're unlucky. You lot do it for the byline."

He inclined his head, accepting the barb with grace. "Why meet me, then?"

I considered the question. The more complicated answer was that it was getting harder to tell who the real villains were, and I needed someone who didn't think in black and white. Someone whose allegiance was to the truth and not to a Syndicate or State.

"Because," I said, "information is my goal, and you are a collector of it. I'm hoping you're open to do a little trade."

He sat back, folding his arms and drawing a line down the center of the table: his side, my side, and the gulf where the truth went to drown.

"All right," he said. "You talk, and if you have something that speaks to me, I'll repay in kind."

"Don't make promises you can't keep," I said, and took the first real drink of the night.

The whisky was better than expected—the kind that burned clean and left a silence in its wake. I let it do its work before continuing.

"You know about the murder at Witcombe Green," I said. "The financier. Auerbach."

Hartwell nodded. "They say it was a robbery gone wrong."

I rolled my eyes so hard I nearly sprained something. "If you believe that, you've spent too long interviewing parliament."

He smiled—there was the reporter's instinct, the subtle twitch that meant he'd found something interesting in the weeds.

"So, what do you think?" he asked.

I leaned in and pulled out the note I found in Auerbach. "I think it was a message," I said, sliding the note across the table to Hartwell. "And I think the person who sent it wants everyone to believe it's just another pogrom, just another warning shot for the immigrants and the Jews. But the truth is, it's more than that."

As he scanned the paper his fingers tapped out a pattern on the table, restless, hungry. "Latin..." He scratched at his stubbled jaw.

"I think," I continued, "the murderer wants someone specific to see what he's capable of. I think it's someone with a sense of theater who meant for the third body, Auerbach's body, to be found before it was exhumed, but they didn't know of the burial practices of the Judaic religion. They had him embalmed, however, with this piece of parchment sewed into the stab wound above his heart."

Hartwell sat with that, the idea percolating through layers of skepticism and surprise. "Do you have a suspect?" he asked, careful to keep the tone neutral.

I did, but saying Blackwood's name wasn't a card I wanted to show him yet. "If I did," I lied, "I'd have brought a priest, not a journalist."

He smiled again, softer this time. "My father was a vicar. I can offer absolution."

"I'll take the whisky," I said, and drained the glass.

I'm told it takes a certain temperament to enjoy the company of journalists. A predilection for pain, or at the very least, an absence of the normal self-preservation instincts. Daniel Hartwell's questions weren't knives; they were a series of gentle, incremental peels, each striping away another layer of resistance.

"You grew up in Ireland," he began. No question mark required.

I nodded, scanning the room. "Limerick."

"And yet you kept the accent. Most try to lose it, especially here."

"My da called it treason to soften a syllable for an Englishman." I swirled the whisky, inhaled, let it torch the back of my throat. "Besides, it's harder to lie in someone else's voice."

He smiled at that, the first honest flicker I'd seen from him all night.

"Any family left?"

The answer wanted to crawl back inside my mouth. "No," I said. "I'd a half-dozen brothers, but they didn't last the Troubles."

A pause. Even the bar seemed to hush itself, as if awaiting the next question.

"I'm sorry," he said, and for once I believed him.

He gave it the appropriate moment before proceeding, all professionalism, no vulturing.

"You're remarkably composed for someone who's seen that kind of loss."

I set down the glass. "You'd be surprised what people get used to."

He studied me then, his gaze moving from the rim of my glass to the half-moon of my mouth, searching for something, a flaw or a fracture.

"Were you close?" he asked. "With your brothers?"

I stiffened, the way a body does right before a needle slid into skin. "Every single one."

His eyes were dark, his expression careful and gentle as he tried to approach sideways. "It must be difficult to live in the country that was responsible for the deaths of your family."

"Some days more difficult than others," I agreed, my tone making it clear I had no intention of elaborating.

He leaned back, letting the silence settle between us. Most people would fill that void with small talk or apologies. Daniel let it harden, a crust forming over the raw bit he'd exposed.

The conversation pivoted, as if by silent agreement, to the case and the disgusting note still nestled in my ruined handkerchief.

"You think it's a message for whomever found him," he asked. "Or for whatever hell he was sentenced to?"

"That's the exact question I have, and I'm not yet close to an answer."

"How did you come to be in possession of it?" He studied me with new perspective, both suspicion and admiration.

"If you think I'm revealing my source, you're mad."

"Was it the Blade?"

I flushed, though I'd die before admitting he'd guessed at least half right. "No! *I* retrieved it from the corpse with my own hands!"

"I hope you washed them since." He wrinkled his nose at the paper smudged and crinkled with the remnants of poor Mr. Auerbach.

He ignored the droll look I sent him, so I said, "I think it was meant to be found by the living, or they wouldn't have placed it so carefully as to not let the message be lost to decomposition. I believe they wanted it found before he went in the grave and didn't think that the coroner would be so lazy.

Daniel seemed to chew the answer, rolling it around in his mind before responding. "Do you think the other bodies also had notes left?"

"I would wonder where, as neither of them had been murdered and adequate autopsies performed."

"Fair point."

I raised my glass to that, then noticed his gaze shift to the bar. Two men had entered, the first in a waistcoat shiny with tobacco oils, the second with a merchant's hands: knuckles like walnuts, nails trimmed to the quick. They exchanged greetings with the barkeep in the kind of low, familiar voices that spoke of routine.

Daniel nodded in their direction. "That's Barnes, the tobacconist, and Loomis, from the hardware shop. They meet here every night after their wives and children are abed. I've made it a hobby to listen in."

"Find anything useful?"

He smiled, conspiratorial. "Depends on your definition. Last week they debated whether the church bell ringer was sleeping with the midwife. Before that, who started the fire behind the bakery. They're the best intelligence in town."

I let him lead the way to a table closer to the bar, but still semi-obscured by a column thick with pub notices and yellowed poems. I positioned myself so I could see the men without being seen, an old habit from the days when a poor angle meant a concussion or worse.

The difference between a conspiracy and an accident was what you overheard in a public house after midnight. I watched Barnes and Loomis nurse their pints, voices dipped just low enough to pretend they were safe from scrutiny. Daniel and I became fixtures at our table: two silhouettes framed by the battered buttresses of Hare and Hounds.

Loomis—hardware merchant, face like a weathered turnip —opened the volley. "I saw it, I'm telling you. They left the poor bastard on Barnes's own step. Throat cut clean through. Police came, took a look, and cleared out before breakfast."

Barnes leaned in, hands trembling faintly as he wiped a ring of foam from his glass. "It's the bloody reverend, I know it. He's got that look—like he'd drown a kitten just to see if it floats. They say he started up a club. Sons of somefing."

"Sons of Albion," Loomis supplied, gaze flicking to the far end of the room as if the walls might be listening. "You know what that is, don't you?"

Barnes shook his head, but his eyes said otherwise.

Loomis dropped his voice lower, forcing us to lean in. "It's like them Yanks have, over in America. Sheets, crosses, the whole lot. Only here it's all bibles and Queen and country. Heard it's for ridding the town of any who don't fit."

Barnes paled. "But the reverend—he's a man of God. 'Sposed to love everyone, inn't he?"

"He's a man of England, first. And we hate what isn't us."

The statement hung in the air, filmy as cigarette smoke, and I could feel Daniel tense beside me. Not with fear, but with the electric thrill of a story snapping into place.

"Pamphlets all over my street," Barnes continued, voice

quivering. "Blaming the Jews for the bank collapse, the Irish for the fires, even the Russians for the damned weather. My wife says our son's not to go to school alone—some foreigner might snatch him up."

Loomis shrugged, bitter. "This world used to be decent."

I looked over at Daniel. His face was sharp, alive with the prospect of a page-one lead. But beneath that, I recognized the set of his jaw—the knowledge that newsprint and blood often came from the same factory.

Daniel's arm brushed mine, a silent signal to store this away for later.

We let the men finish their pint and took our leave when conversation had unraveled into a disagreement about the finer qualities of the tax code. Daniel helped me into my coat before punching his fists into his own after tossing a coin to the barkeep.

"You see?" he said as we stepped into the fragrant early morning hour. "Best intelligence in town."

I nodded. "I can't deny it."

We stood in the quiet for a moment, letting the implications settle.

"So," I said. "What do you plan to do with this information?"

He thought about it, eyes on the ring of light around the High Street's lone gaslight at the main crossroads. "Easy. Use it to find the truth and then to tell it."

"Be careful," I said. "Sometimes the truth gets people killed."

He smiled, rueful. "That's the first thing they tell journalism students at Cambridge." He laughed, and for a moment, we just breathed the same thick air.

There was a kinship in shared risk. Or maybe just an understanding that the world sorted people into two types: those who ran from the fire, and those who ran toward it.

Daniel plopped his hat on his head, and I couldn't help but notice that it made him all the more handsome. "What now?" he asked.

"Now," I said, "we see if we can identify any of these Sons of Albion."

He smiled, the expression brightening the gray edges of his face. "Careful. If you start sounding like a journalist, I'll have to put you on the payroll."

"If you can afford me," I replied, gathering the invisible threads of the night around my shoulders.

Down the thoroughfare and up the acres of hill atop which the Goldsmid estate glowed, the festival music was as drunk as the revelers, but here it was just the pulse of our footsteps and the uncertain path ahead. Daniel peeled off at the crossroads, promising to call if he learned anything new.

I watched him go, his figure dissolving into the mist, and wondered if either of us would survive the next week with our reputations—or our skin—intact.

I turned for home, my mind already sorting the night's revelations into categories: evidence, speculation, the things best left unsaid. There was work to do, but first, I'd need to sleep with one eye open.

However, for the first time in years, I found myself looking forward to the mysteries tomorrow would bring.

Though I wasn't certain if it was because I would be investigating with Night Horse, or because I'd get to share the truth with another dangerous ally named Daniel Hartwell.

Chapter Nine

The second day of the Goldsmids' summer solstice festival was a demonstration in the art of organization. Every inch of lawn had been rolled, shaved, and perfumed into submission, a living rebuke to the threat of weeds or the memory of blood recently spilled on these grounds. Here, under a sky white as a boiled egg, the elite of Buckinghamshire paraded their children, dogs, and unspoken prejudices with equal pride to the rest. The air reeked of tallow and trampled grass, punctuated every few steps by the shriek of a neglected violin or the more pained wail of a child denied a second honey cake.

Celeste and I strolled the promenade, our arms looped more for mutual support than any show of sisterly affection. Night Horse trailed a pace behind, silent as a rumor, his posture erect and hands neatly clasped behind his back—one part valet, one part executioner, depending on who was doing the staring. The effect on the locals was palpable; most parted around us with the reflex of sheep sighting a wolf, while a few looked on with the naked interest of amateur zoologists.

"Were you out late last night?" Celeste murmured, eyes fixed ahead as we passed a trestle groaning beneath the weight of sugar-ribboned pastries.

"I was at the pub with Hartwell," I said. "Eavesdropping on the local lushes."

She hid a smile behind her fan. "How monstrous. Did you discover any delicious gossip?"

"Actually, I did, but we should speak of it away from the public."

Night Horse offered no commentary, though I was acutely aware of his attention. Every now and again I'd catch the glint of his gaze sliding over the crowd, each face cataloged, each threat assessed with predatory efficiency. I wondered if he was bored. Somehow, I doubted it.

We lingered near a tent adorned in the tricolor bunting of what the English considered "continental charm." Inside, a toothsome youth in a blue sash peddled raffle tickets for a commemorative tea set, his accent wavering between Etonian and gutter as he spied Celeste. I let her parry his advances, using the opportunity to scan the perimeter.

It was as gaudy a festival as could be mustered from the imaginations of ex-mercantile nobility. There were sack races, an imitation maypole, a shadow puppet show for the bored children of bored lords, and a petting zoo that consisted, rather implausibly, of Shetland lambs, bunnies, ducks, kittens, and a woefully molested miniature pony. At the far edge of the green, some enterprising soul had set up a shooting gallery, complete with tin effigies of the era's favorite villains —Bismarck, Napoleon, and a moustachioed Russian labeled only as "The Anarchist."

I leaned in toward Celeste, lowering my voice to the register reserved for confessions and criminal propositions. "Hartwell says the Sons of Albion are recruiting in the counties. Their favorite targets are immigrants, East Indians, and Jews."

She pursed her lips, unamused, glancing around at the gathering. "Do you think they're here now?"

"Likely. Men that are beholden to such fraternities are often painfully average in the light of day."

She eyed Night Horse, who was in the process of staring down an entire cricket team. "Poor Aramis, he'd be a likely target, as well."

"Don't underestimate him," I said. "He has a talent for surviving...hostility."

Night Horse appeared at my shoulder so suddenly, I almost inhaled my own tongue. "They've a fraternity like that in the States. A Klan that dresses in white and hunts down former slaves, Natives, Jews, and immigrants alike. They hang the innocent from trees, torture, and scalp the men and—"

Celeste whirled on him. "We cannot discuss such things in front of children!" she hissed.

Said children were a fathom away, but I took her point.

Night Horse's jaw flexed, but he kept his opinions to himself.

We wandered farther, the crowd thickening as we neared the centerpiece of the affair—a massive pavilion housing the main buffet and, judging by the quantity of uniformed servants, at least three ongoing scandals. Night Horse steered us clear, motioning instead toward the animal pens.

It was there, in the shadow of the petting zoo's solitary tree, that I spotted Daniel Hartwell. He was doing his best to blend in, but even out of his pale linen suit he radiated a kind of urban restlessness, as if he were secretly allergic to grass stains and country air. He was squatting next to a crate of ducks; his gaze fixed not on the animals but on a nearby cluster of clucking matrons. I saw him clock us, saw the slight dip of his chin that signaled recognition.

Before I could raise a hand, Celeste tugged me back into the current of bodies. "We cannot be seen to comport with a journalist, I'm the daughter of a Comte!"

"Apologies," I shrugged. "It's England. Journalists are everywhere one finds the wealthy and titled. Like fog, or... syphilis."

We were halfway to the ducks when a commotion erupted at the pavilion. I recognized the high, clear voice of Lady Vronskya, her vowels so round you could roll them down a hill. In her wake came Alexei Vronsky, all youthful arrogance and perfect posture, accompanied by a man and woman whose resemblance to him was matched only by their mutual contempt for each other. The Vronskys were dressed in identical shades of navy, the effect both militaristic and vaguely aquatic.

Alexei spotted Celeste instantly. His face lit up in a way that would have made most girls faint, but Celeste only straightened her gloves and waited for him to close the distance.

"Miss Celeste! You are even more beautiful under the open sky," he said, bowing with a theatricality that would have gotten him beaten in any decent Dublin pub. "And Miss Mahoney—lovely to see you as well."

I favored him with a nod but kept my hands behind my back. Alexei's charm was mostly for show, but his mother— Lady Vronskya—watched us with the cold, steady gaze of a woman who had already calculated the cost of every soul present.

"Miss Beaumont," Lady Vronskya purred, "do introduce us to your companion."

Celeste, ever the actress, slipped immediately into her role. "Ah, yes! This is Mr. Night Horse, my valet and personal manservant. He is American."

Lady Vronskya's eyes devoured him with the polite hunger

of a cat presented with a slow, well-marbled mouse. "American, you say? I have heard it is a wild country. Is it true your people live only for battle and horses?"

Night Horse, unphased, offered a slight bow. "My people lived mostly for surviving the men who wanted our horses. And the battles, they were brought by the invaders. We were a peaceful tribe."

The Lady's painted lips twitched with genuine interest. "How very exotic! The English are so dull by comparison. All wars, but never passion."

Celeste, unwilling to be upstaged, turned to Lord Vronsky, who was already half-lost in the contemplation of the maypole's architectural deficiencies. "You must have seen many countries, Lord Vronsky. Are the Americans so different from the Russians?"

He returned to himself with a start, as if awoken mid-dream. "Americans? They are peasants and defectors with powerful guns to match their greed. Russians—" he paused, as though searching for a memory of home that didn't reek of wet leather and sorrow, "—Russians are different. They have soul, but too much. It burns us up sometimes."

The silence that followed was brittle and exhilarating. Even the wind seemed to pause, unwilling to intrude.

Lady Vronskya, never at a loss, broke it. "And what of the English? How do you find them, Mr. Night Horse?"

He considered her for a full, uncomfortable second. "As far as I've learned, the Russians, Romans, and the British conquer and assimilate. Americans conquer and annihilate." He let the words settle, heavy as grave dirt. "I can't speak to many differences above that."

Lord Vronsky blinked, then nodded slowly. "Yes, yes, this is so. There is no room for anything but power and progress. Those who resist are trampled by it."

Even Celeste looked shaken by the callus nature of Vronsky's dismissal of Night Horse's uncomfortable truth, but she recovered quickly, turning the conversation from a fire to an inferno.

"It must be very difficult," she said, "for those who are not born to power. I have heard there are...societies, here, that protect the rights of the English above all else?"

I cringed at her lack of subtlety.

Lady Goldsmid smiled, a slow, dangerous curl. "You mean the Sons of Albion, yes?"

Celeste affected innocence. "Is that what they are called? I have only heard whispers."

"They are not worth your curiosity. They are thugs, like every other gang of frightened men." Mr. Goldsmid, a large and quiet man made a face, the kind usually reserved for the taste of bad caviar.

Alexei, who had until now kept to the fringe of the conversation, piped up with a shrug. "They are harmless. Talk, mostly. The type of fragile souls who need some nonsense to belong to. Some creed which to follow blindly. They are as stupid in their hatred as they are in their fealty."

His father rounded on him, voice edged with something older than anger. "You say this because you have never crossed them, Alexei. My solicitor—Leo Schulman, he was tarred and feathered for trying to marry an English girl. She was the magistrate's daughter. Now he lives in fear, and she is married to a pig farmer."

Celeste gasped, and I did not doubt her sincerity. "That is barbaric."

Lady Vronskya gave a tiny, exquisite shrug. "England is more barbaric than it admits. But the Goldsmids are clever and garner very few enemies and very loyal friends."

Something whispered to me that she spoke of the Syndicate.

The statement hung between us, obscene and perfectly

shaped. For a heartbeat no one moved, and then Celeste, with the grace of a practiced socialite, changed the subject once again.

"I would so love to see the cricket pitch," she breathed, as though the horrors of ethnic violence could be remedied by a nice walk.

Alexei seized the opportunity. "Come, then. I will show you. Perhaps you will even bring me luck, as you did last night at cards."

He took her arm, ignoring the daggers in his mother's gaze, and led her away. Lady Vronskya followed, leaving Lord Vronsky to trail after, head bowed and hands clasped like a prisoner headed to the block.

Night Horse and I stood in the aftershock, and I glanced up at him with a wince. "I'm sorry if that conversation was out of line."

Night Horse grunted. "She is testing us."

"Lady Vronskya or Celeste?"

He allowed himself a sliver of a smile. "Both."

Across the green, I caught Celeste's eye as she reached the edge of the cricket pitch. She gave a tiny, secret nod—a signal, or perhaps a warning. I pocketed it for later and watched as the day's shadows lengthened across the manicured grass.

Whatever else happened, we were running out of daylight, and I had a growing suspicion that the darkness would be far less forgiving.

THE DETRITUS of festival day was already starting to settle: crushed grass, abandoned bunting, the sticky residue of too-sweet cordials underfoot. The wind, such as it was, had grown lazy, and even the maypole's ribbons drooped in defeat. Night

Horse and I found a patch of privacy beneath the ancient oak that loomed over the west field—a spot the children avoided, perhaps sensing some memory in the wood their parents never bothered to recall.

He stood so close I could hear the shallow, even pull of his breath, the faintest echo of the American prairie breeze in each exhale. His arms were folded, but there was an electric readiness about him, a coil held just at the edge of release.

"Meet me at the kitchen door come midnight," he said, voice low. "I've heard there is a catacomb underneath this estate that used to hide Jesuits during the reformation."

I nodded, rubbing at a patch of honey that had cemented itself to my thumb. "Everyone will still be awake come midnight."

"They won't see us."

I arched a brow. "I'm not exactly built for camouflage, Night Horse. I'm half expecting to turn up at the bottom of a canal by week's end."

He considered this, then shrugged. "We've both survived worse."

It was meant as a compliment, but it tasted sour on the air. We stood in the hush, two figures both defined and disfigured by the things we'd outlived.

He shifted, just enough to block my view of the main house. "The tavern keeper knows more than he admits. He plays both sides, but not well."

"So we bribe him?" I asked. "Or do you prefer the knife?"

He gave the world's smallest smile. "Bribery. Until the knife is required."

For a time, we just watched the shadows lengthen across the lawn. Somewhere distant, the crack of a cricket ball was followed by a ripple of applause—the polite kind, not the real thing. The guests were already migrating toward the tea tents, drawn by the promise of cake and the certainty of gossip.

I thought about Daniel, his quicksilver wit and the way he cataloged the world in glances and scribbles. I thought about Night Horse, and how he saw everything but said nothing unless pressed.

"Why did it bother you?" I asked suddenly.

He looked at me, startled. "What?"

"That I met with Daniel in the tavern. You were angry when I told you. Why?"

He was silent for a long, spooling moment. When he answered, his voice was nearly flat. "Jorah sent me to protect you. He thinks you're too reckless."

I scoffed, louder than I meant. "And what do you think?"

He fixed me with the full, devastating weight of his attention. "I think you know exactly what you're doing. But I also think you underestimate what you mean to—how much of an investment you are to the Hammer. To me."

The admission hung in the air, heavy as a bell toll. I wanted to say something glib, or cruel, or true, but all I managed was: "You're the last man alive who'd care if I vanished."

He looked away, jaw clenched. "That isn't true."

We let the silence sprawl. Around us, the sun dropped behind the first line of trees, painting the estate in gold and ash.

"I can take care of myself," I said finally, softer than before.

"I know," he said. "But you don't have to."

For a heartbeat, I believed him.

From the cricket pitch came a roar, followed by a burst of laughter. The world, it seemed, was determined to return to its proper orbit, no matter how many times we tried to wrench it off course.

Night Horse straightened, rolling his shoulders beneath the battered coat. "At midnight," he said.

"Agreed."

He didn't wait for me to say more. He melted into the dusk, each step so precisely placed I wondered if he'd learned to walk silent for fear of waking all the ancient ghosts buried on our Isle...

Which was once named Albion.

Chapter Ten

I've always found comfort in the midnight hour.

However, the interval between dusk and midnight during the festival was a vibrant tapestry in the country, woven through the hedgerows and thatched roofs, to the gables and gardens, enveloping secrets in a lively embrace that could only be unraveled by revelry. On the second and largest night, the air buzzed with excitement as people gathered in the fields, fired by the glow of lanterns and the rhythm of music echoing across the landscape.

Night Horse stood at the edge of the festival grounds, one boot resting on the grassy knoll, arms crossed, his eyes scanning the lively scene with the keen focus of a hunting raptor.

I joined him, tugging my long, dark velvet overcoat over my bodice. "I know that look," I said, not quite a whisper. "Is something suspicious?"

He didn't turn. "You see that figure?" He raised his chin to direct my notice to a dark-clad specter with a noticeable limp, scurrying around the fairgrounds like a rat who'd pilfered a truffle. "He's looking for something. In the shadows, in large groups, and around every corner. Not once has he so much as glanced at the festivities."

An impossible feat as the castle-high bonfires and drunken revelers could likely be seen and heard across the entire county.

I squinted into the ever-growing crowd, stomach quivering with restless anxiety and eyes watering from a light wind. "Do you think he's here to sabotage?"

"Could be," he said, then looked at me with a glint that could have been mirth or murder. "Or worse..."

We visually tracked the limper as he picked his way through the maze of wagons and bunting, pausing to peek into windows and around columns. When he encountered a bloat of festival goers too dense to navigate, he melted into the background with a skill I envied.

He worked his way toward the far fence line, near the makeshift beer garden that served as the overflow containment for the town's more enthusiastic drunks. Night Horse and I followed, keeping to the perimeter.

He disappeared into the tree line, sidling between two pines where the path cut toward the parish and, beyond that, the rest of Witcombe Green. Night Horse and I paced after him, keeping to the shadows. There was a giddy, animal clarity to the pursuit; the scents of peat, woodsmoke, and fermenting apples muddled together as we left the safety of torchlight and entered the hush.

The path sloped gently downward, dew-slick and rutted with ancient cartwheel furrows.

We trailed the limper as the hedges thickened, our boots sucking at the muddy verge. I would have bet my last farthing that he was either an amateur at stalking, or the boldest professional I'd ever seen. But the moment he passed the bend at the old stone bridge, his limp disappeared—as did the slouch in his shoulders. He straightened, unbuttoned his suitcoat, and upped his pace to a quick, purposeful stride, his steps guided by full familiarity with the pitch-dark track ahead.

Night Horse followed like a dropped bead of ink, staining the air with silence. It might as well have been for naught, as I trotted several behind him, doing my best not to let the heels of my boots or the increasing difficulty of my breath give us away.

We reached the top of the lane where the Catholic grave-yard crowded the back of the church, its stones huddled like guilty conspirators. The figure we'd followed was visible at intervals, a flickering absence more than a presence, but it was enough for Night Horse. He pressed forward, winding through the yew trees, every step calculated for stealth and speed.

As the church's whitewashed brick wall loomed, I lost sight of our quarry.

"Wait," I hissed, but Night Horse was already gone, a shadow among shadows. I cursed him in three languages and hurried after.

Rounding the side aisle, I caught a glimmer of movement in the lee of the vestry. Night Horse was there, poised behind a monument, his eyes narrowed and focused on a gap between the crypt and the sacristy. I followed his line of sight and saw the tip of a black shoe, then the coattail of a man slinking around the transept.

Night Horse flashed a signal for me to stay hidden, ducked low, and charged. He moved with the liquid violence of a hunting cat, covering the ground in a heartbeat and taking the stranger by the collar and the chin. There was a muffled grunt, a brief scuffle, then silence as Night Horse slammed him against the limestone and pinned him with a blade to the throat and a hand across the mouth and nose.

I arrived a couple of seconds later, winded and decidedly noisier than my companion.

Night Horse glared at the wriggling form and shifted his grip. In the blue light of the rising moon, I saw the target's eyes: not the panic of a cornered rat, but the stubborn fury of a man caught cheating at cards.

Night Horse flicked his hat to the ground, exposing the face.

I exhaled, hard. "Hartwell."

The man stopped struggling and blinked, as if waking from a particularly vivid nightmare. Night Horse kept his hand in place, though, regarding the reporter as if deciding between a slice or a stab.

"Stop," I gave in the most commanding of whispers. "Let him breathe."

Night Horse held position a moment longer, then released the grip with a warning pressure. Hartwell coughed, gasped, and then—because he was Hartwell—smirked at both of us.

"Oh good," he rasped. "Mohammad has come to the mountain."

Night Horse's face was expressionless, but I saw his fingers curl, the desire to punch something nearly seismic.

"What are you doing here?" I demanded, keeping my voice below the threshold of echo. "And why were you acting like a proper criminal at the Goldsmids?"

Hartwell straightened his coat and gave me a look that was half apology, half challenge. "I heard talk at the Hare and Hound. A meeting tonight, after midnight, one with violence as its aim. I figured you'd be at the festival, so I came looking to see if you wanted to join my investigation."

"You invite Fiona to a violent gathering without knowing the extent of the danger?" Night Horse growled, low and venomous. "The Sons of Albion consider the Irish their enemy."

Hartwell shrugged, casting me a beatific smile. "I half-expected for her to have been one step ahead of me. I was rushing just now for the thought that she'd taken it upon herself to come alone." Sizing up Night Horse, he turned a disarming conspiratorial wink in the assassin's direction. "Should have remembered she was smart enough to conscript the most lethal man in London as her cavalry. Point of interest...How do you two know each other?"

Night Horse's fist tightened around the blade in his hand.

"Where is this conclave supposed to take place?" I demanded, stepping in to separate them. "We must discover their aim and connect the Reverend to them with enough evidence to convince the most scrupulous of courts. There's little more I detest than an evil man of God."

Night Horse's expression flickered—just briefly, the way a scar might ache in the presence of rain. For the span of a heartbeat, I saw a flash of something not quite guilt but its close cousin, as if he'd been caught playing at a game with loaded dice. Then the mask snapped back into place.

He sheathed the blade, but not without a calculated show of reluctance. "If you want to get yourself killed, Hartwell, that's your business. But you drag her into it, and I'll make sure the next grave in this yard is yours."

"Noted," said Hartwell, massaging his throat with theatrical dignity.

The silence rippled, broken only by the distant hoot of a train and the percussive call of a nightjar. I raked my fingers through my hair, gritting my teeth. "Well then. We're all here. Shall we see what the very worst men in Buckinghamshire do when they think no one's watching?"

Night Horse gave me a look that was equal parts exasperation and something softer, shaded deep beneath the surface. For a moment, he seemed on the verge of apology—not to Hartwell, who was rubbing his neck and muttering, but to me, as if he'd failed to protect me from the sharp point of my own curiosity.

He looked away first, eyes tracing the rough boundary of graves and wild rose, then back at me with a kind of reluctant calculation. "We'll go together, and we go in silence," he said, then shot a look at Hartwell that would have blistered paint. "If you can manage it."

"Lead on," said the journalist, falling into step beside me, close enough that I could smell the cheap tobacco and better-than-average whisky on his breath.

We circled the church, keeping low until the bell tower's shadow lanced the grass. In the stillness, every sound was amplified: the scuff of shoe leather, the faraway pulse of the fair, the faintly musical clank of a farm gate. Night Horse motioned us down, and we crouched behind a line of child-sized tombstones, each carved with the kind of cherub that would haunt a less practical mind.

The men were out there, somewhere. I could feel them—an audience assembling behind a velvet curtain, waiting for the curtain to rise. The air stank of moss and summer blooms, but beneath it there was another smell: the sweet-and-rotten of lamp oil, or kerosene.

"They're not in the church," I whispered. "They're behind it. The crypts, maybe?"

Night Horse nodded once. Hartwell looked at me, curiosity and anxiety sparring in his eyes. "You don't seem surprised," he murmured.

"I'm not," I said. "Men like Blackwood love the theater of it."

We crept closer, using the tilted stones as cover. My knees ached and my lungs burned from the effort of stillness, but I kept moving. Hartwell matched me step for step; Night Horse was already ahead, a phantom picking his way across consecrated ground with the insolence of the truly unbe-lieving.

At the far side of the church, a dull glow leaked from beneath a storm door. Night Horse pressed his ear to the wood, then motioned us closer. I moved up, keeping one eye on the lane and the other on the dark windows overhead.

From inside: a low hum of voices, broken by the snap of a lighter and the unmistakable click of glass against wood. A meeting, then. Men not accustomed to being overheard.

Night Horse pointed at me, then at the door, then at himself. I took the cue and slipped to the opposite side, flat-tening myself against the damp stone and counting my own heartbeat to keep from panicking.

The plan, such as it was, involved opening the door as quietly as possible, slipping inside, and not dying imme-diately.

I'd had worse.

Night Horse waited for a lull, then worked the latch with the delicacy of a surgeon. The door opened inward, slow and noiseless, and we entered a corridor lined with stacks of hymnals and candles. The passage twisted left, ending at a flight of stone steps leading downward.

We followed the voices. At the base of the stairs was a rough-hewn chamber, its walls laced with pipes and ancient roots. Maybe two dozen men stood in a ragged circle, some in Sunday black, others in dark laborers' shirts and mud-caked boots. At their center: a crate, lid pried open, its contents masked by rags.

Blackwood was there. Not in vestments, but in the severe coat and collar of an undertaker, his hair slicked to the skull and his face gleaming with sweat. He addressed the circle with the cadence of a zealot, every word weighted to cut and cauterize.

"We have suffered the foreigner's boot on our necks long enough," he intoned. "Tonight, we strike not just for ourselves, but for England. For every man who cannot feed his family, for every child who cannot pray to the Christian God without fear of reprimand."

A murmur of assent, low and ugly.

Hartwell tensed beside me, fingers white on the edge of his notebook. Night Horse remained still, but I saw his eyes flicking, mapping exits and threats.

Blackwood paced the altar, every line of his body radiating conviction and cold, calculated rage. "The enemy is among us. They buy our land, steal our jobs, defile our bloodlines. They breed in squalor and teach their children to hate everything we are."

His gaze swept the pews, and I felt the collective flinch as he locked eyes with each row.

"They are not content to live in our shadow. They want the light. Our light."

A voice from the pews: "What do we do?"

Blackwood smiled, but it was the smile of a man who'd never once regretted a violent thought. "We show them what it is to be English."

A thunder of fists on wood, a rising chorus of assent.

"They think we're cowards," Blackwood continued. "They think we're weak. That we can be replaced, erased, bred out of existence."

He paused, his eyes burning with the peculiar fire of a true believer. "They forget we have our own history. Our own destiny."

The crowd erupted in cheers, the sound echoing off the vaulted ceiling. My heart pounded so hard I was sure the men in the nearest pews could hear it.

Night Horse's hand closed over my wrist, squeezing until

the bones ground together. I glanced at him, and saw his jaw was rigid with anger. I wondered, for the first time, how many nights he'd spent listening to men like Blackwood debate the best way to eradicate everything he was.

On the platform behind Blackwood sat a figure in a red mask, tall and silent, flanked by two men who looked like they'd been carved from scrap iron. The red mask had no mouth or eye holes—just a blank, anonymous surface, the color of arterial blood.

Hartwell nudged me, breath hot in my ear. "Who's the man in red?"

I shook my head, but in my gut, I knew: the real leader. Blackwood was the voice, but the masked figure was the mind.

"We begin with the Goldsmid house," Blackwood said. "Let them know that their money will not keep them safe from the real English. From those who earned it off the sweat of their backs and paid them with our nation's currency when they have no nation of their own."

There were cheers, not raucous but grim, the sound of men who had practiced hatred long enough to make it feel like duty.

Blackwood let the reaction settle, then cast his gaze around like a lighthouse searching for floundering ships.

As the reverend preached his awful sermon, the man with the red mask almost floated off stage in a swirl of black robes.

"The Goldsmids and their kind have made a mockery of this parish," he continued, his voice a serrated whisper. "They buy land from the bones of our fathers. They turn our churches into meeting halls for mongrels and heretics. Even now, our children are forced to eat, drink, and marry among the sons of Jacob, the daughters of Russia or Prussia, or the bastard spawn of the Irish or Americans."

A man in the back, with the beard and weight of a butcher, raised a fist. "Hang the Irish!" he demanded, voice thick with bitter laughter. "They slip in through every hole, breed like rabbits, and then whine when a proper Englishman puts them in their place."

Blackwood smiled, thin and sour. "The Irish are as much a blight as the Hebrew, though they have the decency to rot from within, not without. Mark it: neither will be satisfied until every Englishman is supplicant in his own land."

A few men spat on the floor in unison at the mention of "Hebrew." Hartwell tensed, and I thought for an instant he might lurch forward and damn the consequences.

Blackwood went on: "We, the Sons of Albion, are not monsters. We are not brutes or beasts, as the gutter press would have you believe. We are the guardians of our nation's soul. We do what is necessary so that our children's children will not speak Russian, Hebrew, French, or Hindi, or that Godforsaken Gaelic at the dinner table."

A ripple of laughter, dark and ugly.

"In the coming days," Blackwood continued, "there will be more funerals. Let them weep and gnash their teeth. We will not be cowed by the enemies of Christ!"

Hartwell whispered, "They're preparing for something. We should go."

But I shook my head. "Not yet. We need to know what they're planning."

The meeting devolved into logistics and threats and the kind of collective bile that passes for courage among men who could not fight alone. They took up weapons and torches like a proper mob as Reverend Blackwood prayed over and blessed them each individually before providing instruction on how to sack the Goldsmid estate.

The fact that they wore such sinister masks to hide their features made their anger that much more demonic.

"We have to warn everyone," I whispered.

"The sooner the better," Hartwell agreed, shifting toward the door, as he was closest.

Hartwell's foot skidded on a loose hymnal, sending it tumbling down the steps with a hollow clatter. The sound of the prayer book hitting stone was like a detonator: all at once, the tension in the church snapped and every head turned. For a few beats, nobody breathed.

Then the men in the pews surged to their feet, the first row vaulting the benches in their urgency to hunt. Blackwood's voice rose above the fray: "Find them!"

Night Horse yanked me so hard my shoulder nearly separated, pulling me behind a column as the nearest goon barreled past.

Daniel Hartwell moved like a ferret, ducking down and grabbing a black mask off a hat rack. He jammed it over his face, squared his shoulders, and plunged down the steps and into the oncoming tide.

"What are you waiting for, you sodden lot?" he bellowed, voice pitched with theatrical outrage. "They went out the back! Get them!"

For a moment, chaos ruled. The pews emptied in a wave, men tripping over each other as they bolted for the exit. Night Horse and I doubled back, winding through the side chapel and out a half-rotted confessional.

Night Horse didn't waste time. He found a door I hadn't seen and shoved us through, slamming it behind. We stumbled into a narrow staircase, the walls slick with condensation and fear.

We hit the night air at full tilt. Behind us, shouts and the pounding of boots. Night Horse set a breakneck pace for the edge of the churchyard, leaping tombstones and vaulting iron railings as if born to it. I lagged, weighted down by skirts, a corset, and a cumbersome coat, but he grabbed my sleeve and hauled me over the final fence, my lungs hot with rage and oxygen deficit.

We tumbled into a drainage ditch, mud oozing up my hem and into my shoes. Only when we reached the edge of the graveyard did I look back. The church glowed like a lantern in the night, the stained-glass windows hiding the true nature of the beast within.

I shivered, remembering the red mask.

How many devils operated from a church?

It surprised me, how easily I fell into the particular rhythm of being hunted: the judder of my heart in my throat, the measured calculation of every footstep, the awareness that behind me, an animal with a hunger for my blood on its tongue was gaining ground. I'd spent years perfecting the art, but tonight, it was elevated to something like worship.

The fields were slick with the approaching morning's dew, each step threatening to pitch me face-first into the mud.

Night Horse never slipped, never slowed, just powered forward as if the earth itself bent to his will. I burned to match his pace, ignoring the ragged tear in my calf and the taste of copper in my mouth.

At the far edge of the first field, we dropped to our bellies and watched the parade of torches as they gave up the hunt for us and reversed their trajectory toward the Goldsmid's hill. Men barking to one another, sharing courage of the liquid kind as they fantasized of violence. They were not organized, but they didn't need to be.

Their purpose was fuel enough.

"We split to warn the household," Night Horse said. "You take the greenhouse; I go for the west gate."

"What if Daniel is discovered," I fretted.

Night Horse's gaze fixed on me, sharp as flint. "He knows what he's doing."

A flare of anger—or something like it—caught in my ribs. "You could at least pretend to care."

For the first time all night, he let himself show a flicker of feeling. "I care that you survive. The rest is...not my business."

It was the closest thing to tenderness I would ever get from him.

Chapter Eleven

We ran.

Neither of us bothered with the pretense of decorum—just the raw mechanics of flight: lungs burning, ankles aching, heart hammering out each second closer to catastrophe. The Goldsmid estate, usually a moon-swept kingdom of hedges and statuary, felt suddenly hostile and alien. Each topiary figure became a threat, every shadow an accomplice to the violence about to be unleashed.

Ahead, the south lawn yawned open, a clearing in which the festival's lesser lights had gathered for a midnight punch-bowl. I half-expected the crowd to part with a gasp as we barreled toward them, but most were too deep in their own vices to register our approach. Night Horse pivoted left, skirting the mass, and I followed, pulse still ragged from the sprint.

We were nearly to the main drive when I caught a flash of movement in the boxwood arcade—a pale hand, then the blur of a gold-tipped shoe. I wheeled, grabbing Night Horse by the sleeve.

"Wait—there," I panted, voice too thin to carry.

He turned, gaze following mine. In the wavering gloom, two figures tumbled out of a garden alcove. Celeste's hair was undone, haloed by mist and moonlight, and she clung to the arm of Alexei Vronsky as though he were both the villain and the cure. They looked, for a heartbeat, like children caught raiding the pantry, lips still damp from whatever secret feast they'd been sharing.

Each other.

Night Horse's eyebrow arched in what I took to be purest disgust, but he said nothing.

Celeste saw us and composed herself with supernatural speed, fingers flying to smooth her skirts. Alexei, less artful, simply blinked, wiped his mouth, and squared his jaw as if expecting a duel.

"Fiona! Aramis!" Celeste called, voice tight. "We were just coming to find you!"

I glanced back toward the church lane. From this angle, the far horizon pulsed with the red-gold rhythm of approaching torches. I'd seen the like before—in the riots of Limerick, and once in a mining town where the miners brought their own apocalypse. It always started this way, with light and noise and the certainty that tonight would not end as quietly as it began.

Celeste's hand crept around his arm, less for protection than for show, and her eyes met mine with a flicker of the old conspirator's fire. "We saw something strange," she said. "At the church down the hill. Lights—more than usual progressing this way. Is it part of the festival?"

"No," I managed, the words brittle as I breathlessly panted my warning. "They're coming for the festival. The Sons of Albion. Blackwood's in front. But there's more. Men. Armed. They're on the warpath."

Alexei's face changed as if someone had drained the blood through his ears. "Why to the festival?"

"They're a nationalist group," Night Horse said, voice flat. "They bring the hatred of foreigners with them."

Alexei opened his mouth, then closed it, then turned to Celeste with a look that bordered on the comic. "We must go inside," he said, and started to usher her up the gravel path with the brisk efficiency of a man who'd once fled pogroms on foot.

But Celeste did not move. "And the people?" she asked. "They'll panic. There are children here, old women—"

"They'll do worse if you don't warn them," I said.

Night Horse scanned the perimeter, gaze slicing through the decorative hedges and rows of glass. "The mob is a quarter mile out. If the servants are clever, they can bar the doors before the first torches reach the portico. That will slow them."

Alexei bristled, but there was no time for pride. "We go. Quickly."

We went.

Night Horse set a punishing pace along the moonlit carriageway, his long legs devouring the ground in strides I could not match without nearly eating gravel. Celeste and I followed in less graceful lockstep, skirts catching on the cinders, shoes slick with dew. Alexei led us through a side corridor I'd never noticed—a tradesman's shortcut used, perhaps, for bringing in ice or hiding bodies.

Inside, the Goldsmid house was its own species of bedlam. Servants scurried from parlor to kitchen, clutching trays of silver and towers of glassware. In the main hall, Lady Goldsmid was directing a platoon of maids, her voice slicing through the panic like a well-sharpened knife. Mr. Goldsmid stood at the foot of the stair, motionless as a ship's mast, his beard still frosted with the remains of his last cigar.

I burst into the entry, Night Horse at my side. "The Sons of Albion are coming," I said, louder than I intended. "From the church. Mob of thirty, maybe more. We have minutes, not hours."

Mr. Goldsmid paled. "The gates—"

"Will not hold," Night Horse finished. "They have ropes and axes. Maybe rifles."

Lady Goldsmid's hand flew to her throat, but she didn't waste time fainting. "Get the children inside," she barked at the nearest maid. "Tell the men to stand ready at the doors and send as many festival goers as possible down the back garden and toward the Vronsky estate. MacKinnon, send for the law."

Alexei and Celeste exchanged a glance so intimate I wanted to slap them both. But to their credit, they turned at once to help. Alexei ran off toward the kitchen, barking orders in a mix of Russian and rough English. Celeste, for her part, seized a candlestick and began lighting every lamp in the main hall, as if their flame, alone, could stave off darkness.

I found myself standing in the foyer, watching as the last traces of normalcy fled from the house like heat from a dying hearth. The echoes of the festival—the laughter, the music, the sticky perfume of spilled punch—already seemed centuries distant. In their place was the cold certainty of the coming violence, the knowledge that tonight we were all equally vulnerable, no matter how thick the walls or how ancient the family name.

Panicked women and children flooded into the grand entry and milled up the stairs. Men with too many pints in their bellies relied on danger to stabilize them to concerning effect.

Outside, the noise built—a swell of animal rage punctuated by the hiss of bonfires and the metallic clang of something heavy striking the estate gates. At first, the festival crowd had assumed it was some elaborate prank. I watched a few children peer from behind the lemonade stall, giggling as the first ranks of the mob burst into view.

It was only when the chanting began in earnest that the laughter died.

Night Horse stood at my elbow, hand resting on the hilt of whatever weapon he'd stashed under his coat. His face was unreadable, but I could feel the tension in his frame, the animal stillness of a man preparing for pain.

Or death.

"I don't understand their hatred of foreigners..." I murmured, fighting back humiliating tears of terror.

"I do," he said darkly.

Chapter Twelve

The next moments blurred, a sequence of shouts, slammed doors, and the thud of boots echoing up from the stone cellar. Mr. Goldsmid had shed the mask of patriarch and now stalked the halls with the white-knuckled terror of a man counting his every prior sin. He corralled servants, barked orders, and clutched a hunting rifle he'd probably never fired at anything larger than a pheasant.

His wife, Lady Hannah, stood statue-still by the French windows, eyes locked on the distant glow of lanterns. For all her steel, her fingers trembled at her throat, twisting a diamond necklace until I worried she'd cut off her own air. "All these people," she whispered, her words fogging the glass. "We brought them here, and now—"

"We organize. We arm ourselves. It's the only way," I said. My voice carried a bite I'd not intended, but there was no point in gilding the moment. As a woman in occupied Ireland, I'd had to go to war in the streets before.

I'd lost my entire family on a night like this.

Night Horse posted himself at the top of the main staircase, a vantage that gave him line-of-sight to every approach, every window, every possible avenue of attack. He'd found a length of iron pipe—God knew where—and it hung from his hand like an extension of his own will. His only other preparation was a roll of medical gauze, which he wrapped tight around his right knuckles.

I turned to find Celeste, but she was already at work, guiding the remaining guests into the drawing room with the speed and focus of a field surgeon. Alexei stationed himself by the door, shoulders squared, jaw set in the way of men who have only ever imagined their own heroism.

"Filth is Foreign!" echoed the masculine, guttural chant. "England for the English!"

Within minutes, the mob had reached the first ring of lanterns. They tore down bunting, smashed crockery, and upended tables as they came. All wore the black masks, faces behind them glistened with sweat and malice.

No sign of the thin man in the red mask.

At the head of the pack, Blackwood raised his arms like an evangelist, his white surplice flaring behind him. "Your day is done!" he bellowed, his voice splitting the humid night. "No more foreign interests in parliament! No more of our wealthy daughters marrying European nobility! No more celebrating satanic pagan rituals! No more!"

"No more!" His cavalry chanted. The line surged, slamming into the ring of lawn where the festival games had been set up. For a moment, the violence was almost childish—ripping the heads off paper effigies, tossing croquet balls through the air, trampling the cake tent into a mess of sugar and blood-orange glaze.

Then someone set the first torch to the ice house. It went up with a boom of steam and shattering glass.

Inside, Lady Goldsmid yanked the curtains shut. "What do we do?" she whispered. Not to me, not to anyone in particular—just to the universe, I supposed, or perhaps to the God she'd long ago traded for diamonds and champagne.

"We hold them off," I said. "For as long as it takes. Help the guests, bar the windows, douse the lights that face the lawn. Shoot them, if necessary."

She nodded, face drawn and suddenly ancient. "We've sent for the constabulary, but they've not arrived."

"They're probably part of the Sons of Albion," Night Horse said.

The guests huddled in the drawing room, the air thick with fear and the sickly sweet reek of spilled port. A few of the men tried to organize a resistance—rolling up sleeves, breaking chair legs for clubs—but most simply sat, hands clasped, waiting for someone else to decide if they would live or die.

I left them and found Alexei and Celeste by the stairs. Alexei had armed himself with a saber taken from the billiard room's display case; he swung it a few times, testing the balance.

"You ever use one of those?" I asked.

He grinned, sharp and reckless. "Only on cabbages and my fencing instructor."

"Then aim for the soft bits," I said. "Heads, hands, anything that's not covered or armored."

He nodded, face settling into something like calm.

Night Horse motioned for me to join him at the top of the main staircase. The first of the mob was battering at the doors, their fists and boots echoing through the marble. Glass shattered in the front hall as a brick came sailing through, spraying the tiles with shards. I felt the familiar rush of terror, that edge-of-the-abyss thrill that came only when you were absolutely certain you were about to die.

"They'll break through in minutes," I said.

Night Horse didn't answer, just adjusted his grip on the pipe.

From below, Blackwood's voice again, howling over the chaos: "Bring them out! We want the Irish whore, the Russian bastard, the Jew-lovers and their spawn!"

A strange calm washed over me. This was not the worst way to die, I decided.

At least it would mean something.

At least I'd spill enough English blood to appease my ancestors.

"They'll want to make a show of it," I said quietly.

"Yes," Night Horse replied, dark eyes glittering with something like anticipation. "They do not know blood is our trade."

Our. His and mine.

With a splintering crack, the front doors gave way. The mob poured into the entry, trampling the runner and hurling themselves at the first obstacle in their path—a heavy oak barricade wedged by the butler and two footmen. The footmen held as long as they could, but the weight was too much; they scattered as the crowd surged up the stairs.

Night Horse stepped forward, his silhouette framed in the landing's soft gaslight. He waited until the first masked man came into view, then brought the iron down, shattering the man's arm with a single, surgical blow.

The man screamed and toppled, taking two others down with him. The mob paused, the animal logic of pain overriding their collective bloodlust for an instant.

Alexei joined in, saber slashing in quick, precise arcs. He had a knack for it, after all. I spotted one man go down, clutching his side; another staggered back, shrieking as the blade grazed his face.

I picked up a chair from the landing and swung it over the

rail. It struck one of the masked men square in the head, and he folded like bad origami.

"Good," Night Horse grunted, already back to work.

The mob pressed on, but the narrowness of the stairs worked against them. Every time they gained ground, another body tumbled back down, and the landing grew slick with blood and sweat.

A lull. The next wave hesitated, unsure. These were not warriors or soldiers, only rural rabblerousers too cowardly to show their faces.

"Now," Night Horse hissed.

Alexei and I barreled down the steps, flanking Night Horse, and together, we drove the front ranks back into the foyer. The noise was deafening—screams, the wet thunk of metal against flesh, the hiss of someone letting loose with a bottle of acid or lye.

In the chaos, I caught sight of Blackwood at the rear. He raised a pistol and aimed, but his hands shook. The shot went wild, shattering a mirror.

Night Horse didn't flinch. He vaulted the last few steps, landed in the mob, and turned the pipe and his blade into instruments of retribution.

He was beautiful like that, elemental and unyielding. For a moment I simply watched, my own body irrelevant, the architecture of violence as inevitable as the dawn.

Then I remembered how little martyrdom paid, ripped the leg from a chair, and waded back in.

At some point the chaos found its rhythm—a sick, exhilarating pulse. I lost track of whose blood was whose, if the shrieks were terror or rage or simply the soundtrack of history repeating. Hands grabbed at my coat, fists aimed for my face, but the mass of bodies worked against the mob as much as for it. Night Horse held the top of the stairs, reducing every would-be hero to a whimpering lump before they could clear the landing, and Alexei made a game of tripping the rest as they tried to retreat.

I expected the crowd to thin, to realize they'd bitten off more than they could chew, but the black masks kept coming. The front ranks were already slicked with the afterbirth of violence; the ones behind seemed determined to drown in it.

Without warning, the tide broke. A new clamor rose outside, closer than before, and for a wild moment I thought the constables had finally arrived.

Then I saw them, streaming past the shattered gazebo and trampling the elegant peonies: townsmen, shopkeepers in their nightshirts, dairywomen with rolling pins, even the vicar, who looked ready to bludgeon heresy with a borrowed croquet mallet.

They'd come back.

The refugees that Lady Goldsmid had "evacuated" out the back had returned, picking up sticks and stones and whatever else the English countryside offered for weaponry. The women had raked their hair back and stomped the grass flat in their march; the men, faces bare and flinty, approached the Sons of Albion with the clear-eyed, stubbornness that I'd always admired in the Great British underclass.

The effect on the Sons of Albion was immediate. The second rank, never so brave as the first, tried to reverse course into a wedge of their own bodies. In the crush, I heard Blackwood's voice again, now shrill, "Hold your ground!" But his own men were already falling back, buoyed by the pure force of their own panic and the growing certainty that, contrary to every instinct, the "filth" fought back.

Night Horse spotted Blackwood as he tried to melt into the press of bodies, his white collar now a liability, not a banner. "There!" he shouted, and Alexei, face streaked with blood and triumph, surged after him. The two cut a path through the melee, Night Horse's pipe and Alexei's saber working in tandem, a brutal ballet. I tried to follow, but my ribs shrieked in protest where a bruising fist had landed.

I scanned the landing, looking for Celeste, and found her wedged against the banister, knees buckled, face slack. For a moment I thought she was dead, but then her eyes flickered up, desperate and full of terror.

"Get up," I hissed, half-dragging her to her feet. "We're winning."

She looked over the carnage, mouth slack, then set her jaw and nodded—once, an executioner's nod. "I'm fine," she said, though she clutched at her elbow as though it was in pain.

"Of course you are," I lied, and we staggered after the others.

The Sons of Albion had broken ranks entirely, most of them pushed outside, splitting around the Solstice fires. The gentility of the countryside—those same people who an hour ago debated the merits of strawberry trifle and the proper etiquette of engagement parties—now formed a living wall in the drive. They wielded hedge shears, cricket bats and even a rusted hatchet that had surely not seen action like this.

They weren't just fighting for the Goldsmids or the Vronskys, not really—they were fighting for themselves, for the right to define who belonged without a man in a dog collar telling them otherwise.

The Sons of Albion, exposed and cut off from their strength, did what all cowards did when the tide reversed: they ran. The old trick of the mob was that it rarely wanted to kill, only to prove it could, and once the illusion of invincibility was gone, the bravado leaked out faster than the blood.

I watched Blackwood, robes streaked with mud and blood and less noble fluids, try to rally his men. But they scattered, boots slipping on the churned grass, masks lost or flapping from desperate hands. One or two even threw themselves at the mercy of the townsmen, who accepted their surrender with all the magnanimity of a debt collector at quarter day.

It was over in minutes. The doors of the house held; the windows bristled with faces, not terror anymore but the creeping euphoria of those who'd survived a disaster by standing where they were told. The wounded among the mob howled for a doctor; the wounded among us did the same, but with less drama and more irony.

I was an idiot to allow myself to breathe.

I should have known it wasn't over.

We were just starting to clear the wounded from the lawn when a shriek cut through the early morning hours—thin, wild, the sound of someone who'd run out of words for their terror. A footman came barreling up the path, one hand clawing at his own cheek as if he'd found a spider there and couldn't scrape it free.

"There's a dead man in the side garden," he managed, eyes white as boiled eggs.

For a moment, no one moved. An old woman in a shawl clucked her tongue, muttered something in Hebrew, and went back to searching the grass for her lost dog. The rest of us—already hollow from the night's carnage—could only stare in disbelief.

The footman caught Mrs. Goldsmid by the arm, helped her toward the French doors. Mr. Goldsmid followed, still clutching his unloaded rifle as if it could be of use. I glanced at Night Horse, who met my look with a frown. Celeste and Alexei hovered at the fringe of the crowd, her hand squeezing his so tightly it looked like she might break bones.

The garden was a mess. Lanterns lay smashed in the hedges; the remains of cakes, creams, and meat pies squished underfoot. Flowers and hedges had been trampled.

The body waited for us in the shadow of the boxwood alcove.

He was middle-aged, English, dressed for the city in a suit that would have cost a week of my not-so-meager wages just to brush. His head lolled at an impossible angle, and yet the garden bed beneath him was free of blood. There was no sign of a struggle, no defensive wounds on the man's hands.

The others recoiled, covering their faces or crossing themselves, but I forced myself closer.

Night Horse hovered at my shoulder, eyes raking the hedgerows for any sign of movement.

I knelt, reaching for the corpse.

The pockets had been turned out, and the left cuff torn and covered with grit.

A shadow passed over me. I looked up to find Celeste, pale as death, staring at the body with an expression of perfect horror.

"We were just—" she started, then faltered. Her hand rose to her mouth, trembling.

Alexei put an arm around her, but she shook him off, stumbling toward the hedge. "We were right there," she gasped, pointing at the arbor a few feet away. "The entire time we were...He was just..."

Her knees buckled. She pitched forward, and Alexei barely managed to catch her before her head met the flagstones.

Chapter Thirteen

✦❖✦

T he dead have their own language.

I'd spent years becoming fluent in its subtle grammar—the vocabulary of lividity and rigor, the syntax of wounds and decay. This corpse spoke with an accent I recognized.

This body was a period at the end of a longer, more sinister sentence.

After making certain Celeste was being looked after, I knelt beside him, my skirts pooling around me like spilled ink. Dawn threatened the eastern sky, casting a sickly pallor over the trampled flowers and scattered detritus of last night's festival. The man who'd found him stood trembling by the hedge, making the sign of the cross over and over, as if repetition might scrub the sight from his memory.

"Give me some room," I said to no one in particular, and the circle of onlookers withdrew a pace, all except Night Horse, who hovered at my shoulder like a guardian angel with questionable methods.

The corpse was middle-aged, his features unmarked by

distinction—the type of face you'd pass on the street without registering. His clothes were plain, simple cotton and wool, entirely unsuitable for a festival amongst the aristocracy. More telling was what lay beneath his fingernails: not the clean half-moons of a gentleman, but crescents of soil so deeply embedded they appeared almost black in the morning light.

I unbuttoned his coat with practiced efficiency. The fabric was damp but not from dew...but something older, mustier.

"He wasn't a guest," I murmured to Night Horse. "And he's been dead for at least a day."

Night Horse grunted his agreement, then shifted slightly to block the view of Lady Goldsmid, who had drifted closer, her face a marble study in controlled horror.

I turned the man's head gently, and there it was—the ligature mark circling his neck like a macabre necklace.

With practiced hands, I opened his shirt. The puncture wounds were there too, three of them in a neat line across the lower abdomen. Like the others, the third was deepest—a killing thrust rather than an exploratory one. But again, differences emerged. These wounds were less precise, the edges ragged as if the blade had been twisted or the victim had struggled.

"Is it the same as the Auerbach?" Night Horse asked, his voice so low only I could hear it.

I nodded, then shook my head. "Yes and no. Same signature, but... sloppier. Or deliberate variations to make it look like someone else's work."

I leaned closer, inhaling the scent of the corpse. Beneath the expected odors of soil and decay was another note, sharp and chemical—formaldehyde.

Another embalming.

The burial, too, suggested an amateur's work. He'd been

barely covered, the soil disturbed in a way that spoke of haste rather than reverence. And when I peeled back the edge of his shirt to examine the chest wound more closely, I found the stitching pattern on what remained of his shroud. The technique was different—cruder, using a type of twine I'd not seen before.

"What do you make of it?" Lady Goldsmid's voice cut through my concentration, brittle as frozen lace.

I looked up at her. Her elaborate coiffure remained impeccable despite the night's upheavals, but beneath it, her face had drained of color, leaving only two spots of rouge that now seemed garish against her pallor.

"Someone went to great lengths to make this look like a continuation of the terror this body-snatcher intends," I said, keeping my voice neutral. "But there are discrepancies that suggest either a different hand or a deliberate attempt to confuse."

Behind her, the servants had gathered in a tight knot, whispering behind cupped hands. I caught fragments: "...just like the financier..." and "...a warning, it must be..." and most tellingly, "...the Jew. Or maybe he's Russian..."

Lady Goldsmid swayed slightly, and one of the maids darted forward to steady her. "This cannot be happening," she said, more to herself than to me. "Not here. Not now."

I returned my attention to the body, noting how the limbs had stiffened in an unusual position—arms slightly raised, as if he'd been trying to shield himself at the moment of death. This wasn't the typical pattern of rigor mortis; it suggested the body had been positioned after death, then allowed to stiffen before being moved again.

"He wasn't killed here," I said, standing up and wiping my hands on a handkerchief that had already seen too much service in the past twenty-four hours.

Lady Goldsmid pressed a trembling hand to her mouth. "Why do they leave their dead here? What have we done?"

I didn't answer immediately. The truth was too unsettling to voice aloud: someone had specifically chosen to deposit this corpse at the Goldsmid estate, during their festival, on the very night when tensions had already erupted into violence.

A message of hate written in flesh and blood. Had someone used the chaos to plant the body? Or had it been here for hours and no reveler noticed?

"We need the police. A coroner, at least...a real one," I said at last, though I had little faith in the provincial doctor they'd scare up.

The whispers behind us grew louder, and more servants appeared at the garden door, drawn by the commotion. The news was spreading through the estate like infection through a wound.

Soon, panic would follow.

Finger pointing.

More violence.

Night Horse touched my elbow, a silent signal. "We should prepare," he murmured. "This will not end here."

I nodded, looking once more at the dead man's unremarkable face. In death, he had become significant—a punctuation mark in someone else's gruesome narrative. And I had the distinct, unsettling feeling that we had only read the first chapter.

I watched as the garden filled with bodies—the warm, breathing kind—each new arrival adding to the centrifugal force of panic. Servants, guests, and curious onlookers materialized from every door and path, their eyes widening as they took in the tableau: the corpse, the trampled roses, and me— still kneeling in the dirt like some macabre gardener tending an unexpected crop of corpses.

The whispers swelled to a crescendo, fragments of speculation weaving into a paranoid tapestry. A footman retched into the hydrangeas. Two maids clutched each other, their knuckles white against black uniforms. The gardener who'd made the discovery sat heavily on a stone bench, head in hands, muttering what sounded like childhood prayers.

Night Horse positioned himself between me and the growing crowd. Through the press of bodies, I spotted the Vronskys approaching, Lady Vronskya's face a mask of aristocratic disdain barely concealing genuine fear.

Alexei greeted them, his arms still around the unsteady Celeste, his boyish features had hardened overnight into something more calculating, more cynical.

"Is *this* how the English protect their guests?" Alexei's father demanded, his accent thickening with emotion. "First a mob, now murder?"

Lady Goldsmid flinched as if struck. "This is hardly our doing, Lord Vronsky."

"But it is your responsibility," he pressed, eyes flashing. "My family came here at your invitation. We left the safety of our connections in Russia to strengthen ties with your household and your adopted country. Was it worth it? To risk our reputation—our very lives—for this alliance?"

The question hung in the air like gunpowder smoke. I watched Lady Goldsmid's composure fracture, hairline cracks spreading across her patrician façade.

"How dare you," she said, her voice rising to a pitch I hadn't thought possible from such a controlled woman. "After everything we've done to accommodate your family—the special meals, the Russian musicians, the introductions to London society—you stand in my garden and question the value of our friendship?"

Her hands trembled violently, and she clasped them together as if the pressure might keep her from flying apart.

"Samuel!" she called out, scanning the crowd for her husband. "Samuel, where are you? This has gone quite far enough!"

Celeste had regained her feet but sagged heavily against Alexei, her face ashen beneath its light dusting of powder. Her eyes fixed on the spot beside the rose trellis, not far from where the body lay.

"He was there," she whispered, the words barely audible. "He was there the whole time we were..." She trailed off with a visible shudder, and I didn't need her to finish the sentence to understand what she meant. The alcove where she and Alexei had been caught in an intimate moment—close enough to touch the dead man had they reached out.

Alexei tightened his grip on her waist. "This is intolerable," he muttered, but his eyes darted nervously, no longer those of a man in control.

I rose to my feet, brushing soil from my skirts. "The body has been here for some time," I announced, hoping clarity might dampen the rising hysteria. "He was not killed during the night's attack, but I think was placed here before, and was supposed to be found during the festival. Does anyone... recognize the fellow?"

My attempt at reassurance only redirected the panic. A portly shopkeeper—one of the festival vendors who'd spent the night sheltering in the kitchen—pointed a thick finger toward Lord Vronsky.

"This sort of thing never happened in our village before," he hissed, his jowls quivering with conviction. "Foreign anarchists have been sewing chaos across the country. Now they've followed you here, bringing their violence to our doorstep!"

Lady Vronskya drew herself up like a cobra preparing to strike. "How typical of English narrow-mindedness," she retorted, each syllable dipped in venom. "When something goes wrong, blame the foreigners. Have you considered this might be one of your homespun political vigilantes instead? We all know who controls the banks, who profits from chaos."

The crowd recoiled, then surged forward, voices rising in a tide of accusation and counter-accusation. I caught fragments: "...Irish troublemakers..." "...Jewish plotting..." "...Russian conspiracies..." "...Sons of Albion were right all along..."

My knuckles whitened around the handle of my bag. I'd seen this before—the contagion of fear transforming neighbors into enemies, reason into blind prejudice. And somewhere in this garden stood the actual murderer, watching their handiwork unfold with satisfaction.

"That's quite enough," came a clear, authoritative voice from the edge of the crowd.

The sea of bodies parted, revealing Daniel Hartwell, or a grim facsimile of him. He approached with the confidence of a man who believed his press credentials made him bulletproof.

"Everyone. I understand your fear. It's natural to look for someone to blame." His gaze swept the assembly, lingering briefly on the most vocal accusers. "But consider this: whoever left this corpse at a festival attended by people of various nationalities and faiths might have been trying to manufacture just such a rift among neighbors. Such a malefactor's greatest weapon isn't the bomb or the knife—it's the fear and division that follows."

A hush fell over the garden. Daniel stood tall, unintimidated by the collective weight of suspicion now directed at him.

"The question isn't which group is responsible," he continued. "It's who benefits from turning you against each other. Who profits when the Goldsmids no longer sponsor the Vronskys? When English shopkeepers refuse to serve Jewish customers? When Chinese immigrants are driven from their homes and the Irish are starved out of their own farms?"

The silence deepened. I watched Daniel—this man I barely knew yet somehow was beginning to trust—redirect the crowd's fear with nothing more than carefully chosen words. It was masterful, and for a moment, I allowed myself to hope it might be enough.

Then Lady Goldsmid's voice cut through the stillness: "And who are you to lecture us on unity, Mr. Hartwell? A man who makes his living from sensationalism and scandal?"

The tension in the garden coiled tighter, now focused on Daniel. Night Horse shifted closer to me, his good hand flexing. Whatever temporary peace had settled over the crowd was already dissolving, like morning mist burned away by the rising sun.

And beneath it all, the corpse waited, patient and terrible in its stillness.

Lord Goldsmid materialized from the crowd like a vengeful specter, his earlier shock calcifying into something harder and more dangerous. His eyes—bloodshot from a night without sleep—fixed on Daniel with the particular loathing the aristocracy reserves for the press. "You," he said, jabbing a finger toward Daniel's chest, "have no place here. This is a private tragedy, not fodder for your newspaper."

Daniel didn't flinch, though I noted the subtle tightening around his mouth. "With respect, sir, murder is never private. Especially when it might be connected to a larger pattern."

"Pattern?" Lord Goldsmid scoffed. "The only pattern I see is your persistent intrusion where you're not wanted."

He turned to a pair of footmen who hovered uncertainly at the edge of the gathering. "Remove this man from my property. Immediately."

The footmen stepped forward, their faces blank masks of servility that couldn't quite hide their reluctance to touch a gentleman, even one as professionally distasteful as a journalist. I moved between them and Daniel, summoning every ounce of the clinical authority I'd cultivated over years of commanding rooms where death was the primary guest.

"This is hardly the time for your sensationalist reporting, Mr. Hartwell," I said, my tone crisp and professionally dismissive. But I held his gaze long enough to communicate something different: caution, not rejection. The subtle widening of his eyes told me he understood.

"I merely wish to be of service," Daniel replied, matching my formal tone. "As someone who has followed the recent... incidents...in the area."

Lord Goldsmid's face flushed a dangerous shade of puce. "Service? Your kind of service we can do without. First the mob, then this"—he gestured toward the body—"and now you, circling like a vulture!"

I turned to face him with the calm certainty that comes from having seen worse—much worse—than an aristocrat in a temper. "Mr. Hartwell may have insights valuable to the investigation, my lord. Before dismissing him, perhaps we should hear what he has to say."

Lady Goldsmid touched her husband's arm. "Samuel," she murmured, barely audible. "Perhaps..."

He stared at her, betrayal written across his features, but fell silent.

Daniel seized the moment, approaching the body with careful, deliberate steps. He didn't touch it—he knew better than that—but crouched to study the details with an intensity that reminded me of Inspector Croft at his most focused. The crowd watched, suspicion warring with curiosity on their collective faces.

"Look at the soil patterns on his clothes," he pointed out.

"It's not presumptive to assume the body was moved from another graveyard not here in Witcombe Green."

A collective intake of breath rippled through the crowd. Lady Vronskya's fan snapped open, a sharp report like a pistol shot.

Lord Goldsmid's face had gone from red to white in the space of a heartbeat. "What nonsense," he sputtered, but the words lacked conviction.

He'd informed the crowd of what I'd already surmised. The mud beneath the fingernails didn't match the rich, dark soil of the Goldsmid rose garden. The dampness of the clothing came not from dew but from being buried in wetter ground. Even the position of the body—awkward, unnatural —suggested it had been transported and deposited.

Daniel continued, warming to his theme. "The state of rigor mortis, the soil compaction on the back of the coat, the particulate matter caught in the hair—he was pulled from a shallow grave, I'd wager, not a nicely appointed coffin."

He gestured toward the man's right shoe, where a smear of reddish clay stood out against the black leather. "That red clay is not from anywhere on this estate."

The crowd murmured, some faces skeptical, others frightened, but all now focused on Daniel rather than on their mutual suspicions.

"There are three graveyards within walking distance," Daniel said, his reporter's instinct for narrative taking over. "The Anglican churchyard, the Catholic cemetery behind St. Mary's, and the Jewish burial ground just beyond the eastern woods."

He pointed to the stitching visible at the corpse's collar. "This man was buried according to Jewish rites, or at least an approximation of them. See the simple shroud, yet notice the preservation—he has been embalmed, which is unusual."

I leaned closer, examining the stitching pattern with new

understanding. It wasn't crude work, as I'd initially thought—it was different, deliberate, part of a tradition I wasn't familiar with.

"Since no one has died in the village recently and no one stepped forward to claim their deceased kin," Daniel continued, "it must have come from somewhere else. Someone exhumed this man from a cemetery and brought him here. The question is: why?"

The silence that followed was heavy with implication. I saw understanding dawn on several faces—the realization that this was not a random act of violence but a calculated message.

A statement made in human flesh.

"How do you know all this?" Lord Vronsky asked, his voice rough with suspicion.

Daniel's smile was tight. "I covered the East End synagogue desecrations last year. I spoke with many rabbis about their burial customs."

I could see the reluctant respect dawning on some faces, mingled with lingering distrust. Daniel Hartwell might be a journalist—a profession generally held somewhere between actors and pickpockets in the social hierarchy—but his knowledge was undeniable.

"If what you say is true," Lady Goldsmid said slowly, "then who is using the dead as a prop in some ghastly theater? What message are they trying to send?"

The crowd shifted uncomfortably. I caught Night Horse's eye across the garden; his slight nod confirmed he'd reached the same conclusion. Whatever game was being played here, it was more complex and more dangerous than a simple murder.

And we were all, willing or not, now players in it.

As a sliver of daylight bled into the sky, Lady Goldsmid straightened her spine and addressed the assembled onlookers with the brittle authority of a woman holding herself together through sheer force of will.

"This has gone on quite long enough," she declared. "Samuel, instruct the steward to lead everyone inside. We shall continue this discussion in the drawing room, away from..." She gestured vaguely toward the corpse, now covered with a sheet that gleamed ghostly white in the gathering dusk.

No one argued. The Goldsmid name still carried enough weight to command obedience, even from those who had spent the day casting suspicious glances at the family. We filed through the open French doors into the house, a solemn procession trailing the scent of crushed roses and fear.

Gaslight flickered against walls covered in intricate patterns of burgundy and gold in the drawing room, while ancestral portraits gazed down from heavy gilt frames with the superior expressions of those who had died before witnessing their descendants' humiliation. A marble fireplace dominated one wall, its mantel cluttered with silver-framed photographs and Dresden figurines that seemed obscenely frivolous in the current context.

Lady Goldsmid paced before the hearth, her silk skirts rustling with each turn like dead leaves in an autumn wind. The sound emphasized the silence that had fallen over the assembled guests, each absorbed in private calculations of risk and blame.

"This cannot continue," she said at last, her voice brittle with barely contained fear. "Three bodies and counting...We must send to London for Scotland Yard."

The pronouncement fell like a stone into still water, ripples of reaction spreading through the room. Most nodded in relief; a few exchanged uneasy glances.

Alexei Vronsky, I noticed, went perfectly still, his eyes

darting toward his mother and father with unmistakable alarm.

"The local authorities are clearly out of their depth," Lady Goldsmid continued. "We need professionals to handle both the murders and the civil unrest. Samuel, you have connections in London—use them."

Lord Goldsmid nodded, a muscle twitching in his jaw. "I'll send for Inspector Aberline. He handled that business with the Mortimer diamond discreetly enough."

"Very wise," murmured the Anglican vicar, who had appeared from nowhere to join our grim gathering. "Scotland Yard will restore order."

I confess, my feelings regarding Detective Aberline were deeply conflicted and yet, on balance, almost affectionate, if only for the sorry kinship we shared in failure. The man had the sharpest mind in Whitechapel, a knack for sifting sense from the cesspit of London's criminality, and a personal flavor of dour compassion that, for all his reticence, practically radiated through the walls of every public house and police station he frequented. And yet, our mutual history haunted us both.

Jack the Ripper.

The very phrase was a dirge, a private requiem known only to those who'd witnessed the aftermath of his artistry— if such a word could be applied to a species of evil so refined, so precise in its cruelty. Like detectives in a Greek tragedy, Aberline and I had circled the same blood-slicked alleys, interrogated the same trembling witnesses, pored over the same anatomical peculiarities that marked each new murder as the work of our elusive nemesis. Each time, we found ourselves a step behind, outmaneuvered by a force that operated with surgical detachment and, worse, philosophical amusement.

But if Scotland Yard was sending Aberline, it meant the

gravity of the case had finally staggered even those marble-faced mandarins in London. It meant the murders weren't just rural curiosities but ripples in a much larger, darker tide. I wondered whether the Ripper's ghost would follow Aberline into Witcombe Green, whether we would, together, find ourselves re-enacting a final act that had begun years ago among the gaslit horrors of Whitechapel. The idea filled me with equal measures of dread and anticipation.

Across the room, Alexei leaned down to whisper something in Celeste's ear. Her eyes widened slightly, but she gave no other reaction. Whatever he'd said, it wasn't good news.

Night Horse drifted to my side, moving with that uncanny quiet that always made me suspect he was only half composed of matter. He watched the conversation swirl around the fireplace, the alliances being forged and broken with every brittle exchange of words.

"I'm going to find out who in the county has joined the Sons of Albion," he said, low enough for no one but me to hear.

I blinked. "Now?" There was a finality to the way he said "find," as if the act itself prefigured an ending by his blade. "You're not planning to do anything...murderish, are you?" I murmured, aware of the bruised hush that had settled over the drawing room, and of Daniel's gaze ticking between us with nascent suspicion from across the room.

Night Horse's eyes slid over mine, unreadable. "That is up to them." He nodded to me before he vanished, leaving a Night-Horse-shaped hole at my elbow and a subtle drop in the room's ambient threat level.

Two servants appeared with trays of brandy and sherry, distributed with the automatic efficiency of those trained to believe that alcohol is the universal solution to all of life's difficulties.

I declined the offered glass and drifted toward the

window, where Daniel stood slightly apart from the others, scribbling furiously in his notebook. His face was animated with an almost feverish intensity, the look of a man assembling pieces of a puzzle that had eluded everyone else.

"Found something interesting?" I asked, pitching my voice low enough that only he could hear.

He glanced up, startled, then smiled—a quick, private expression that transformed his face from merely handsome to something more compelling. "Several things, actually. The body, the burial, the timing—anything but random. But have you considered why someone would go to the trouble of digging up a body from a non-local cemetery?"

I frowned, turning the question over in my mind. "To implicate the Goldsmids and their community, for a small place there are only so many semi-fresh corpses available."

"Perhaps," Daniel said, his pencil tapping against the page. "Or perhaps because this particular body contained something worth recovering—or hiding."

He flipped back several pages in his notebook, revealing a careful sketch of the dead man's hand, with particular attention paid to a mark on the inside of the wrist—a small, circular scar I had noted but dismissed as inconsequential.

"I've seen this before," Daniel murmured. "It's a brand used by a particular group of anarchists operating out of Eastern Europe. They mark their couriers this way."

I stared at him, reassessing everything I thought I knew about Daniel Hartwell. "You recognize anarchist brands on sight?"

His smile was rueful. "I spent six months undercover with the London cell last year. Nearly got myself killed for a front-page exposé no one remembers now."

Across the room, servants hurried to and fro, preparing the house for the arrival of Scotland Yard. Lady Goldsmid had collapsed into a chair, her composure finally fracturing under the weight of the day's events. Lord Goldsmid stood protectively beside her, one hand on her shoulder.

The Vronskys huddled near the door, their faces drawn with worry.

Everyone was playing a part in this grim theater. The question was: who had written the script, and what was the final act meant to reveal?

Chapter Fourteen

❦

The following day passed in a flurry. I slept until noon, then woke to help the household set to rights after so much destruction, then tended to an overwrought Celeste until after dinner.

I escaped to my room with a notebook and my thoughts as early as I could. Once I'd gone cross-eyed, I gave up. I was brushing my teeth with a powder that tasted of burnt clove and baking soda when I saw Night Horse moving across the moonlit edge of the estate.

I watched him from the little casement window above the washstand, froth still on my tongue. He had an assassin's grace and a mourner's patience. Each step was calculated, as though the very grass beneath his feet might give him away. But not to me. I'd spent enough nights shadowing bodies— dead or otherwise—to know the difference between a man escaping and a man hunting.

I spat the last of the powder, slipped out of my night-dress, and into my least conspicuous walking attire: dark skirt, old boots, and my brother's old fisherman's vest. My hair fell wild, so I wrapped it in a scarf and tied it tight enough to give myself a headache.

It was after two in the morning by the time I slipped out the servants' door. The humidity of late June pressed at my skin, the air so quiet and thick it felt like being wrapped in a cheesecloth. The aftermath of last evening's violence hung over the grounds: trampled grass, the soft clatter of a wind-rolled lantern, the faint chemical tang of burning fuel from the put-out torches.

I found Night Horse's trail with little effort. He didn't bother masking his passage—half the time, I wondered if he enjoyed the theater of being followed. The moon was half-shuttered by cloud, just enough silver to make the garden hedges look like the backs of sleeping beasts.

He took the long way around the estate, cutting behind the walled kitchen garden and through a thicket of gooseberry that snagged at my skirt with sticky fingers. I cursed under my breath but kept on. The chill on the air was strange after the crush of the drawing room; it focused the mind, made every sound more urgent. Somewhere, a fox screamed its joy into the darkness. I half wished I'd brought a weapon.

Night Horse led me past the edge of the green and up a narrow lane that shone like bone in the moonlight. The church, when it came into view, was a scab of black against the lighter field beyond. Catholic, of course; the only kind with both the resources and the arrogance to build on a rise so prominent that it could see for miles in every direction. I kept my distance as he circled the building, eyes scanning the graveyard with its tipsy stones and sleeping saints.

He stopped at the side door, listening. He waited there for a long time, motionless except for the soft twitch of his hand at the inside of his coat. I could have called out, but something told me not to. Instead, I slipped closer, using the shadows of the outbuildings for cover, until I was near enough to hear the slow, deliberate cadence of his breath.

He moved inside, leaving the door ajar. The invitation was implied, not extended. I accepted anyway.

Inside the church was a darkness thick enough to drink. The windows leaked moonlight in sickly blue patterns, and the air was layered with incense and old beeswax. I followed the sound of Night Horse's boots on flagstone, heart galloping despite every effort to slow it down.

He stood in the aisle, back to me, head tilted as if consulting the dead. His presence was a black hole; even the candles on the altar seemed to gutter in deference. I took a step, then another...

And he was on me.

I didn't see him move—one instant he was a silhouette against the nave, the next he was at my throat, hand crushing my windpipe and slamming me into the cold stone wall.

I gasped, taste of soap and blood in my mouth. He pressed his body against mine, pinning me with the full length of his arm, and only then did his face register recognition.

"Fiona," he said, the syllables rough-edged. He didn't let go. Not at once.

His eyes were as bright as I'd ever seen them, pupils wide as a cat's. Up close, I could smell the sweet oil he worked into his long hair, the sweat from his sprint, the gunmetal reek of his rage.

"You nearly got yourself killed," he said, voice low. "Why did you follow?"

I had to cough before I could answer. "Because I'm not an idiot. You walk out in the middle of a murder investigation with no word to anyone, I assume you plan to create another corpse or find information I need."

His grip eased, but not enough for comfort. "You shouldn't be here."

"I live for places I shouldn't be."

He looked at me for a long moment.

"What are you doing?" I asked.

He turned his head, scanning the shadows beyond the pews. "Looking for the priest. Thought maybe he'd try to return before Scotland Yard arrives. But he's not so stupid."

I listened but heard nothing but our own breathing, the tick of cooling metal from the candelabra, and the faint tremor of the church's old bones settling.

"He'd be a fool to return here," I whispered.

"I think he's a fool and coward. And this is where cowards hide."

I tried to step around him, but he kept his arm against my chest, holding me in place. "You should go."

"Why?"

He released me suddenly, so abruptly, I staggered and caught myself on a broken pew. "Afraid?" he said, and for the first time in my life I heard him laugh. A dark, unsettling sound that lanced through me like lightning.

We made our way down the aisle, side by side but not together. Every now and again I caught a reflection of my own face in the brass, pale and wolfish, and wondered when I'd become the sort of person who broke into churches for sport.

We checked the vestry first—empty, though someone had recently dusted the chalices and rearranged the altar cloth. The priest's private rooms were also vacant, but I noted the faint impression of a body in the old armchair, and the smell of whisky strong enough to knock a nun sideways.

In the sacristy, Night Horse found a book of sermons and thumbed through it, pausing to study the notations in the margins. He read in silence for a minute, eyes flickering. Then he snapped it closed and looked at me.

"What did you expect to find?" I asked.

He shrugged. "Some men can't help confessing, even when they know it's pointless."

We checked the rest of the church—the cloisters, the crypt, the kitchen. Nothing but the residue of ritual and the dust of centuries.

At last, back in the nave, Night Horse sat on the edge of a pew and stared at the altar as if daring God to blink first.

I hovered by the baptismal font, tracing patterns in the dust with the tip of my boot.

"You ever been to confession?" I asked, breaking the silence.

He glanced at me, dark hair fallen across one eye. "No. I do not believe in sin. Just choices and their consequences."

I nodded, feeling the weight of my own catalog of failures, betrayals, and cowardices. "I like that," I said.

We sat like that for a long time, neither of us willing to break the hush. Outside, the wind picked up, rattling the stained glass. For a heartbeat, I wondered if we'd ever leave, if this was where all stories ended—in silence, waiting for an answer that would never come.

The church looked different in the hour before dawn. The candles were guttering on the altar, dying with a noise like distant weeping. The night's chill was giving way to a thin, predatory light that slithered through the stained glass, painting the pews with wounds of red and blue and funeral gold.

We lingered in the nave, neither of us eager to return to the living. Night Horse prowled the perimeter, slow and restless, his steps echoing with the self-assurance of a predator denied its quarry. I watched him from the front pew, letting the cold from the stone seep into my bones. It felt better than the warm numbness I'd been cultivating for the past week.

"So," I said. "Here we are again, searching for a villain in a Catholic chapel."

His gaze cut to me on a sharp intake of breath.

We never spoke of it, the night he killed my former fiancé. The moment he took revenge for the hand Aidan had in the decimation of America's tribes.

I felt the urge to touch his hand, to draw him closer, but it passed. "Do you find pleasure in killing religious men?" I asked. The question hung between us, luminous and ugly. We'd both promised never to ask, never to force the other's scars into daylight.

He took a long time to answer. When he did, his voice was rough with something I didn't recognize. "Yes. I'm thirsty for holy blood," he said, daring me to contend with him. "Because men like Fitzpatrick, like Blackwood, like every monster that wears a collar or a crown—none of them believe the world can hurt them despite their savagery. So, I show them it can."

His fingers traced the seam between two pews, the motion slow, almost tender. "My people had a name for the God of Abraham. They called him 'the Father of War.' Because every time his followers came, they brought only murder and fire."

I listened, absorbing the shape of the confession. "You think he's behind all this," I said. "The Christian War God?"

"I already said I don't believe in gods, but those who do love to kill in his name." His gaze was on the altar now, the candles licking the shadows into grotesque shapes. "When the Yanks came for my people, they didn't just kill us. They made us pray before they did it. Promised us heaven if we renounced our own gods. Told us it was Manifest Destiny, as if they'd been given the deed to the world by the god who loves only the winners."

His anger was a physical thing—alive and electric, pushing at the air until my teeth ached. "They cut my father's hair, made him kneel, shot him in the back of the head. Then my wife...then my...child... That was my first lesson in Christian charity."

I couldn't look at him. The colors from the windows danced across his face, red and violet and bruise-blue, a martyr lit from all sides. "I would hate them all," I said.

He nodded. "I return their charity in kind."

I remembered the taste of incense on my tongue, the cold press of the confessional booth against my spine. I remembered how many times I'd told myself I was different from my family, that I'd escaped the violence that built our little corner of Ireland. But every story came back to the same altar, the same stain.

The same man on the same cross who never told his followers to love those who are not like them.

Night Horse stood, and for a moment I thought he might strike the altar, smash the candles, tear down the icons with his bare hands. Instead, he leaned forward, palms on the rail, and said, "If God is real, he's a butcher. And I'll keep killing his priests until he comes down to stop me."

His voice echoed through the nave, high and thin and wild. I felt a surge of something I hadn't allowed myself in years—pity, maybe, or just the kinship of two people who'd built their entire lives on the foundations of other people's cruelty.

I wanted to comfort him, or at least to lie and say that things could get better, that the world wasn't just a factory for producing more and better monsters. But the words wouldn't come. Instead, I watched the light move across his hands, coloring them red and gold like a king from a storybook.

"Tell me of your brothers," he said. "Tell me of your loss."

He looked back at me, and for a moment the mask fell away, and I saw the boy he'd been before the world broke him.

"My father and my five brothers, hanged in a row from lamp posts. Every single one of them. I found them swinging, blue and swollen, still dripping, and the youngest—Fayne—he was fifteen and wore my scarf because he said it smelled better than sheep or gun oil. He was still wearing it when they cut him down."

The words tumbled out. "They left a sign—said God wouldn't let them into the real heaven, the Anglican one. And I knew, even then, that the same sign hung over every house in our street, every window with a Mary in it, every peasant that ever prayed in Latin. The Protestants killed the Catholics, the Catholics did the same, and in the end, it was only the crows who kept a tally."

The church behind us seemed to grow colder, as if the stones were drawing in their breath, waiting for the next blow.

"I don't believe in God," I said, "but I know what a war god looks like. He lives in every man who tells you to choose a side or die."

We stared at each other, our chests filling as if we'd run a league.

Night Horse made a sound, low and broken. For a moment I thought he'd speak, but instead he tilted his head back and screamed.

It was a sound like nothing I'd heard—part howl, part yelp, part the purest fury a body can channel into noise. It cut through the morning, ricocheted off stone walls.

He screamed again, higher this time, a shriek that would have made the angels piss themselves. He whooped and hollered, curses and names and what must have been prayers in a language I'd never heard, and then he crashed through the confessional door and began tearing the world apart.

The statues fell first. Saints and virgins and the gaudy, lacquered Christ who always seemed one insult away from blinking. Night Horse knocked them down with abandon, all the while whooping and screeching in a dance of destruction that held me transfixed.

He moved to the icons, slashing them from the walls with a blade that seemed to appear from nowhere. He cut the ropes on the bell, then stood under it and bellowed until his voice was gone. He flung candlesticks at the altar, tore open the baptismal font and spit in it.

The violence was...ceremonial. Each act had meaning. He performed them not as desecration, but as communion— making the church a mirror of his own ruin.

And then he stopped, panting, face streaked with sweat and soot and something that looked suspiciously like tears.

He looked at me, and I saw not the assassin or the wolf or even the broken boy from the prairie. I saw a man who wanted so badly to have faith in anything, he would rather destroy the world than admit he was empty.

I did not know what to do. So I did the only thing that made sense. I walked to him, took his face in my hands, and kissed him as though we could burn the past out of each other.

He returned it, desperate and sharp, mouth hungry and bruising. He pressed me against the altar, hands roaming, teeth at my jaw, and I let him. I wanted the pain, the reminder of being alive. I wanted to feel my heart racing, to feel his body solid against mine, to be reduced to something so simple and clean that there was no room left for ghosts.

We fucked like animals—or like things haunted by the memory of animals—right there in the ruins of the sanctum, among the shattered icons and toppled saints and the sour puddles of sacramental wine. The air still burned with the ozone of his fury, and each time our bodies crashed together, another avalanche of votives or statuary rained down from the altar, as if the old gods, insulted by our trespass, demanded their own orgiastic destruction. I barely remembered the process of unbuttoning, unfastening, undoing. His coat stayed mostly on, my skirt hiked up in a grotesque parody of Sunday best; we clutched and tore at each other with the panic of the freshly drowned, desperate to breathe through the other's mouth, to vanish inside a skin that wasn't our own.

He was rough, not out of cruelty but because gentleness had no place in a place like this, not anymore. I bit his shoulder hard enough to draw blood, and he laughed a wet choke of surprise, then bit me back, his teeth at my throat, the mark of the wolf written indelibly above my pulse. My hands found his ribs, the old scar tissue there, and traced each lump like a rosary, naming a litany of new and unpronounceable saints: Sorrow, Fury, Shame, Want. His fingers were at my hips, my thighs, the small of my back, everywhere at once, bracing me against the cold edge of the altar as he drove into me on a rhythm older than language. I could feel the jagged grit of broken glass grind into my knees, the sticky seep of wine and blood and tears gluing us to the stone, but I would have let him break every bone in my body if it meant we could keep tearing ourselves loose from the world for one more second.

We did not speak. There were no endearments, no whispered names, only the obscene monosyllables of flesh, the slap and suck and shudder of bodies determined not to survive themselves. At one point he grabbed my face in both hands, thumbs crushing hard against my cheekbones, and looked right through me, his eyes black with need and loathing and something perilously close to awe. I hated him for it, and I loved him for it, and I wanted to crawl inside him and make myself a new home where no memory could ever find me.

The climax, when it came, was not a single moment but a rolling, seismic collapse—his hands bruising my hips, his mouth at my ear, the taste of iron and incense and rage on my tongue as I let myself be reduced, atomized, rewritten in the language of mutual ruin. For a few seconds I thought the world might actually end, that the foundations of the church would give way and swallow us into the waiting earth, and for the first time in years I almost hoped it would.

When it was done, we lay tangled on the cold stone of the altar, letting the silence fill us back up as we contemplated our pleasure and our blasphemy.

After a time, he spoke. "You know the first thing I learned to do as a child?"

"What?"

"Skin a deer. My grandfather told me: if you want to know a soul, cut it open and count its rings."

I laughed a little, but tears dripped into my hair. "How many rings do I have?"

He rested his forehead against mine. "Enough to last a hundred winters."

The light through the windows shifted, growing softer, more forgiving. For a brief, delirious second, I thought maybe the world could start again, that we could build something new from the char and the dust.

But I knew better.

We left the church as we found it: emptied of answers, heavy with the memory of blood.

We walked back to the estate in silence; our shadows stitched together by the dawn.

In my room, I stripped out of my ruined clothes and stood by the window, shivering, not from cold but from the certainty that I would never again fit into any world that expected order or kindness. Night Horse took off his boots, sat on the edge of the bed, and looked at his hands as though surprised to see them still attached to his body.

He did not try to touch me, not at first. But when I crawled into bed, still dressed except for my shoes, he slid in beside me, and we lay together like two logs in the aftermath of a fire, spent and silent, the world finally quiet around us.

He held me, and I held him back, and together we waited for the morning to come.

Chapter Fifteen

I was glad Night Horse had left my room before I woke.

He would have scoffed at the curses I spat when I watched Grayson Croft prowl the Goldsmid estate from the shadowed comfort of my window seat, eyes still stung raw from the previous night.

What in the ninth circle of hell was Croft doing in Buckinghamshire? I thought they'd sent for Aberline.

The inspector moved with the wary grace of a man who'd had the uncouth street urchin trained out of him by years of bureaucratic trench warfare. His hat sat low and punitive on his head; his coat, though pressed, had already acquired the half-life of a thousand similar investigations, the lapels bitten at the edges by memory and rain. He was taller than I remembered—or maybe the English countryside had simply shrunk.

He made a circuit of the grounds with the same methodical energy I'd once watched him use to dissect a barroom brawl: mapping, cataloging, ruling out. Where the hedge was trampled, he knelt to inspect the bruised leaves. Where a window was broken, he ran a forefinger along the glass, collecting a sample like a parish priest lifting the Host. His notebook appeared and disappeared with the rhythm of a magician's trick. Not an extra word written but the exact truth.

He paused at the garden, at the patch where the body had lain, and looked up as if he could see me behind the linen and the leaded glass. For a second, I thought he'd try to spot me out, but instead he just fixed his gaze on some middle distance, jaw working, working, grinding out whatever was left of his patience with the world. Then he straightened, pocketed the notebook, and strode toward the front entrance, shoulders squared and marching for a reckoning.

It didn't take long for word to reach me. The butler, a man bred for discretion and later broken of the habit, found me not two minutes after I'd seen Croft disappear through the double doors. "Inspector Croft requests your company, Miss Mahoney," he said, voice as flat as the linen napkin in his breast pocket.

I thanked him and rose, smoothing the wrinkles from my skirt and counting down the seconds until I had to face the man I once called colleague—and, for a season, an intriguing prospect.

He wouldn't be happy to see me, and I became incomparably glad I hadn't surprised him.

Croft hated to be surprised, probably because very little was capable of the feat.

The main hall was all echoes and ancestral disapproval. The portraits lining the staircase stared down, mute witnesses to every social transgression, each frame an unbroken chain of disappointment stretching back to the Norman Conquest. Croft waited at the foot of the stairs, hat in hand, one boot tapping out a measured tempo against the tile. He wore the uniform of the Yard, which meant his tie was only slightly crooked and his badge of office glimmered in the afternoon gloom like an accusation.

I made him wait, just long enough to reestablish the balance of power, then descended with all the dignity I could muster.

"Inspector Croft," I said, offering a hand.

He took it with a perfunctory squeeze, eyes never quite meeting mine. "Miss Mahoney."

We stood there, momentarily unsure whether we were enemies, allies, or simply relics of each other's worst memories.

"You've come from London?" I said, breaking the spell. "We expected Aberline."

He nodded. "Took the early train from Marylebone. Even with the rush, the news of last night's events beat me here by several hours. The superintendent thought it prudent to dispatch a more..." He searched for the word. "A detective more adept at keeping order in a crowd."

I smiled, though I doubted he saw the humor. "I suppose you qualify."

He exhaled through his nose. "You have a gift for understatement."

Croft cut the figure of a man who'd been built for war and accidentally found himself working for the law. He was Yorkshire stock—thick wrists, knuckles like a butcher's block, and the kind of jaw that made lesser men reconsider their convictions mid-sentence. The fine stitching of his coat had surrendered at the shoulders, straining against the mass beneath. Even his posture—bolted spine, deliberate in stillness—spoke of violence carefully rationed, meted out only when the Queen's peace so required.

His eyes, though: those betrayed him. I'd always remembered them as the bleak blue of sleet, but recent years had chipped away at them, leaving rings of exhaustion and something older, sadder, around the iris. It was the look of a man who'd buried more friends than he'd made, who expected the world to serve up another betrayal with each sunrise.

He clocked me head to toe in a single, all-consuming glance. "You look well," he said, and I almost laughed. The last time we'd been in a room together, I'd confessed to lying about the death of his nephew. To call things complicated was like calling the Thames a bit damp.

"Shall we?" He gestured toward the smaller salon, a room so overburdened with velvet upholstery and porcelain curios that even the air seemed to move with caution.

We took seats opposite, the table between us littered with the detritus of yesterday's high society: a collapsed bonbonnière, a tea service already cooling, a deck of playing cards mid-hand, as if abandoned at gunpoint. Croft pulled out his notebook and clicked a pencil into readiness.

"I understand you were present during the incident," he began, tone all business.

"I had the poor taste to attend the festival, yes."

He ignored the sarcasm, flipping open to a fresh page. "Walk me through what happened."

I recited the basics, careful to remain factual but not overly helpful. The Sons of Albion, the torches, the general air of motivated ignorance. How the crowd split, how the servants and guests barricaded themselves, how the townsfolk finally found their nerve and rallied. I left out the violence that happened inside my head and bones, and the extent to which Night Horse had protected me, or I him.

Croft's pencil never stopped. The questions came in crisp succession, each designed to box me into a smaller and smaller corner:

"Who first raised the alarm?"

"Who gave the order to bar the doors?"

"Did anyone else besides yourself see Reverend Black-wood's involvement?"

I answered as best I could, flavoring each reply with just enough truth to pass muster. He never looked up, but I saw the minute twitches of his jaw when I mentioned Night Horse's presence, the pulse in his temple each time I refer-enced the criminal element.

He'd never know how we'd sinned on the altar of God.

At last, he snapped the notebook shut. "And the body in the garden?" he asked. His voice was softer now, almost disap-pointed.

I shrugged. "I found it after the fracas died down. Male, forties, killed elsewhere and moved here. Not a festival guest, not a local, not—at first glance—relevant to anything but someone's idea of a sick joke."

His hand hovered over the notebook, fingers drumming in a slow tattoo. "You're certain he wasn't one of the Sons?"

"He was not one of them," I said, and let him stew over whether I meant the mob or the cryptic Jewish brotherhood whispered about in the drawing rooms of Whitechapel. "He'd been dead before they even met that day."

He hesitated, squeezing the bridge of his nose. "You always did attract corpses."

"Nature abhors a vacuum," I replied.

The air between us was brittle now, charged with all the things we'd left unsaid the last time we worked together. The years in between hadn't dulled his mind, but they'd carved new channels of doubt and regret into his features.

He shifted in his seat. "Forgive me, but I must ask: what is your relationship to Mr. Night Horse?"

I met his gaze, and for once he didn't look away. "Profes-sional," I said. "We have mutual interests. That's all."

He nodded, but I could see he didn't believe me. "He's dangerous."

"So am I."

"If I find that you're working for the Syndic—"

The moment was broken by the arrival of Samuel Goldsmid, who swept into the salon with the bracing confidence of a man accustomed to solving all problems with the right application of money or threat.

"Inspector!" he said, clapping Croft on the shoulder. "I trust Miss Mahoney is being as helpful as ever?"

Croft stood, professional mask in place. "She's been invaluable, sir."

Goldsmid turned to me, eyes glinting. "The house is indebted to you, Fiona. Should you require a testimonial—"

"Thank you," I said, and rose before he could finish the sentence.

Goldsmid steered Croft toward the library, leaving me alone in the echo of their departure.

I let out the breath I'd been holding and wandered the hall, fingers trailing the banister as if searching for a new direction.

Only later, as I replayed the conversation in my mind, did I realize Croft had never asked why I was at the festival in the first place.

Perhaps he already knew.

Chapter Sixteen

The rest of the afternoon was a blur of servants picking glass from the rose beds and overwrought houseguests comparing scars. Lady Goldsmid had retreated to her room for an indefinite period of "rest," which left the main corridors eerily quiet. I found myself drifting, half-certain Croft would reappear to quiz me again, but he seemed absorbed with the family patriarch, the two of them locked in the kind of grim conversation reserved for men who equated the loss of property with mortal wound.

I wandered the house in the aimless pattern of the professionally suspicious, keeping one ear tuned for the telltale cadence of Croft's boots or the more measured step of Night Horse, should he have found his way back indoors. Instead, I found only dust, old carpet, and the uneasy silence that settled over a house once the violence had passed and all the witnesses were too ashamed to relive it aloud.

It was in the east corridor—a wing lined with watercolors and poor taxidermy—that I spotted the first symbol. At first, I mistook it for some flaw in the joinery, a knot of wood or careless overpainting, but the longer I stared, the less accidental it seemed. The curve was too deliberate, the sharpness too fine. I ran my thumb over it: a stylized mark.

I'd seen it before. Half of it, at least, the sigil stamped on the outside of the paper I'd found in Mr. Auerbach's stab wound. On the spine of his ledgers, stamped in wax on a bottle of stolen absinthe, even etched into the bone handle of the knife he kept in his desk drawer.

It was the sigil of the Syndicate.

Jorah's mark.

I felt the hairs on my arms stand up, cold prickling my skin despite the house's stifling humidity. I pressed harder, half-expecting it to give or trigger some mechanism, but the wood remained stubborn and inert. When I pulled away, I noticed another symbol, several feet farther down, carved into the baseboard next to the door of an unused parlor.

A trail.

I followed it, pulse ticking up in my throat. The marks repeated at irregular intervals, sometimes low on the wainscoting, sometimes tucked behind the ornate whorls of a radiator cover. None would have been obvious to anyone who didn't already know what to look for, and even then, only in a house as absurdly old and overdecorated as this one.

The trail led me, inevitably, to the library.

The Goldsmid library was legendary, an architectural riot of spiral staircases and floor-to-ceiling shelves all hand-carved and dusted with the arrogance of the truly unread. The carpet was so thick it dampened every footstep, and the fireplace was big enough to cremate a horse without breaking a sweat.

But today, all I saw was the panel of wood to the left of the hearth, inlaid with a gold sigil identical to the ones in the corridor, only this one was meant to be found.

I checked over my shoulder—no Croft, no Goldsmid, no

lurking servant with a tray of unnecessary sherry—and crept to the panel. I touched the mark and found it cool and slick, as if the metal never fully acclimated to the ambient warmth of the room.

I pressed it. Nothing.

I slid my nail along the edge, felt a catch, and then—on a hunch—pressed the gold inlay inward while pulling gently to the left. There was a soft click, almost polite, and the panel slid open a finger's width.

My first impulse was to close it, walk away, and pretend I hadn't seen anything. My second was to go back to the kitchen, make a strong cup of tea, and hope Night Horse showed up to talk me out of doing something reckless.

Instead, I reached for the lamp on the side table, a little bronze monstrosity shaped like a neoclassical nude holding aloft a flame. I checked the oil, found it half full, and struck a match with hands that only trembled a little.

The passage was narrow, just wide enough for a person to slip through sideways. The air on the other side was cool and close, tinged with a mineral odor that suggested stone or earth, not just dead air. I ducked my head and entered, the lamp first, then my right shoulder, then the rest of me in a careful shuffle.

The panel closed behind me with a hush of felted gears, locking out the light and the world and leaving only the uncertain flicker of the lamp to guide my way.

For the first time since arriving at the Goldsmid estate, I felt something like fear. Not of violence or mobs or even the supernatural evil that always seemed one step behind me in my old life, but of this: the knowledge that I was stepping directly into Jorah's world, and that the only way out was through.

✦

THE PASSAGE SLOPED DOWNWARD ALMOST at once, narrowing and roughening as the smooth wood gave way to old stone, the walls closing in with each step. The air grew colder—the sort of damp that belonged not to the climate, but to a history of bad decisions and secrets best left unsaid. The lamp's flame sputtered in the draft, its faint light chasing the shadows down the spiral with a kind of canine eagerness. I trailed my fingers along the slick wall, counting each turn, each damp outcropping, every trickle of condensation that had formed in these depths long before the Goldsmids had even considered building their fortune above it.

At the bottom, the passage leveled off, terminating in a black iron door set flush with the rock. The handle was simple, almost modern—a lever, not a knob, as if the Syndicate's appreciation for subtlety stopped where efficiency began. I tried the handle. It gave without complaint.

The chamber beyond was small, no larger than a minor gentry's breakfast nook, but dense with the accoutrements of criminal bureaucracy: a heavy desk, battered but oiled to a shine; two tall filing cabinets painted a flaking government gray; shelves crammed with ledgers, folders, and what looked suspiciously like several bottles of spirits tucked behind a row of archival boxes. The place reeked of mildew and old receipts. It was at once less and more sinister than I'd expected.

I shut the door behind me, pulled a scarf over my nose, and let the lamp play over the surfaces. At first glance, the desk was nothing but an explosion of paperwork, every inch a battleground between order and entropy. But there was a method to the chaos, and within minutes I found the first clue: a letter, half-folded, the wax seal broken but still bearing the impression of that same Syndicate sigil.

The letterhead was Goldsmid's own—stamped in blue and

gold, written in a hand that oscillated between the baroque and the bureaucratic. The contents were, at first, unremarkable. Pleasantries, condolences, vague threats veiled as business advice. But halfway down, my breath caught:

"...per our agreement, the shipment will arrive at the usual place, but the schedule must accelerate due to the increased activity in Whitechapel. Trust the Hammer to handle all necessary arrangements, but keep the ledgers concealed. Even the smallest inconsistency and the entire enterprise collapses. Roth will not tolerate a second warning..."

The letter ended abruptly, as if the writer had lost nerve or been interrupted. But the point was clear: this was not merely a matter of dirty business. This was blackmail, collusion, a chain of command that started at the Goldsmid breakfast table and ended in the kind of backroom deals that built and broke governments.

I thumbed through a drawer at random. More letters, this time on stationery from various East End banks, all addressed to S. Goldsmid or, more often, to a code name: Ozymandias. Each letter bore a different hand, but all referenced shipments, collections, or "liquidation events" in the same careful phrasing. There were deposit slips, many stamped with London's more reputable banks, the numbers obscene. In the margins of one ledger, I found Jorah's name written and circled, with the annotation: "Red Queen. Do not engage directly."

My hands were shaking now, a tremor I tried to smother by gripping the edge of the desk. It was one thing to suspect the Goldsmids as facilitators of Roth's criminal enterprise, but quite another to find proof that they were the fulcrum on which the entire operation balanced.

I set the lamp on the floor and scanned the shelves, looking for anything that might indicate a ledger of names, a kill list, some evidence of the bodies the Syndicate left in its wake. Instead, I found a battered file marked with the sigil. I didn't need to translate much to understand that these were dossiers on "troublesome elements." At the top of the list: Alexei Vronsky, then a few pages later, the Vronsky patriarch, and then, in the English section, a long profile on none other than Jorah David Roth.

The Hammer.

I expected depravity. I expected violence, a diagram of blood or a ledger of debts signed in veiled threats and initials. What I did not expect, and what stilled me with a chill so sudden I nearly dropped the lamp, was the file on Jorah Roth himself: a dossier so thick it could have been a modest novella, bound in cracked oilcloth and crammed with memos, police sketches, even the odd amateur rendering by a witness too frightened to sign their name.

I opened it and found, at the very front, a portrait: not a photograph, but a pen-and-ink rendering that captured Roth in profile, the jaw cut from the grain of memory and the shadow of malice. Even the artist, who I guessed was police, had not been able to deny a certain intelligence in the line of the mouth—a hint of humor, or perhaps a private joke between the face and the watcher.

The dossier was divided into epochs, as if Jorah had been born and reborn a hundred times, each with its own set of grievances, debts, and unfinished business. The earliest entries were in Yiddish and Russian, painstakingly translated in red ink by some underpaid clerk. They described a boy orphaned in the Pale, smuggled into England among the refuse of a failed revolution, and emerging in the lime-lit alleys of East London with nothing but a name, a talent for violence, and a genius for organization. The next years were a parade of small gangs and larger betrayals, each described with clinical precision by the Yard or the local constabulary. He started as a knife for hire, then a collector, then a broker of information so potent it nearly got him killed by the age of twenty-five.

There was a note about his knack for surviving what should have been fatal reprisals. Bullet wounds, knife wounds, at least two poisonings. In each case, the attached medical report was followed by a witness statement describing Jorah. They'd had a difficult time chasing him at first, he'd arrived with a forged passport and a name that was never quite the same from one census to the next. There were mugshots from the 1870s, each more confident than the last, and reports from constables who swore they'd seen him orchestrate a dozen rackets before he'd turned twenty. One particularly dog-eared page described a riot in Spitalfields, attributed to a "pale youth with wolf's eyes" who set fire to a rival's bakery only to return an hour later and help the fire brigade put it out. "He was laughing," the report read. "He was the only boy I've ever seen laugh while watching London burn."

The later entries were in English and they read like the minutes from a parliament of devils. Jorah's ascent mapped like the trajectory of an invasive species: carving out territory in the East End, neutralizing rivals not by brute force but by bribing or blackmailing them into a doctrine of mutual survival. He'd absorbed Jewish gangs, then Irish, then Chinese, creating a web of influence, violence, and money that stretched across the entire civilized world.

I was still thumbing through the Hammer's file—reeling, if I were honest, from the neatness with which my entire understanding had just rearranged itself—when the faintest tickle of air brushed the nape of my neck.

It was followed, within seconds, by the unmistakable sound of footsteps from the corridor above. Two sets, their rhythm offset: one heavy, measured, and almost theatrical in its attempt at discretion; the other quick and just this side of panicked, as though its owner had spent his life being the second through every door.

Every nerve ending prickled with instantaneous terror.

This cavern and its endless shelves stored everything the Syndicate held on its own people...

And I was about be caught with information that would see me at the top of the Syndicate's kill list.

I doused the lamp, the sudden dark so complete it felt like a second skin. There was no time to hide the evidence, so I did the next best thing: I knelt beneath the desk, wedging myself into the narrow shadow. I slowed my breathing, counting heartbeats, and tried to remember if the door had made a sound when I let it settle back into place.

The footsteps grew louder, and with them, voices—low, the consonants ground to dust in the hush of the underground. I caught the accent before the words: Russian, but not Vronsky senior. Alexei, then. And the other voice, bright and elastic, barely contained by the need for secrecy, belonged to Daniel Hartwell.

For a full thirty seconds they hovered just outside the door, their conversation a hissed jumble of English and Russian filtered through the wide mesh of a criminal's ear. I made out fragments: "...no, you said it was here..." "...like the others, this one is dangerous."

I did not breathe. I did not allow myself even the luxury of a swallow. In the pitch dark, my senses recalibrate: the chemical tang of old typewriter ribbons, the iron-filings scent of lamp oil, the faintest under-odor of male sweat—one sharp as gin, the other sour-edged and anxious. The doorknob rattled, then stopped. The heavier set of steps retreated half a pace, as if to guard the hallway. The lighter ones—Alexei, I'd bet both my own and his mother's fortune—drew a single, hesitant breath just outside the threshold.

A key scraped metal. The lock clacked open.

Light flooded the room, electric and jaundiced.

I pressed tighter into the shadow, muscles rigid, every cell waiting for the inevitable.

Chapter Seventeen

✦❀✦

The light sliced the dark like a surgeon's blade, laying the cramped chamber open for dissection.

I pressed so deep into the shadow behind the desk, limbs wrapped around my own ribs to keep from shuddering. Two shadows filled the threshold, momentarily fused in silhouette: one slim and confident, the other upright, coltish, and slightly too young for the world it was about to inherit.

Alexei Vronsky entered first, followed by Daniel Hartwell, the latter carrying a battered tin lamp whose thin beam dissolved all the secrets the room might have otherwise kept. They moved to the center of the chamber, careful to stand in a patch of relative cleanliness between two heaps of moldering ledgers. The smell was fierce—a bouquet of rotting paper, stale spirits, and something older, cellular, the air thrumming with the memory of a thousand secreted confessions.

Alexei turned and shut the door with a quiet finality, then set his back to it. "Did anyone clock your entry to the house," he said, his voice barely above a whisper.

Daniel set the lamp on the desk; dust motes leapt to existence in the sickly circle of illumination. "No one did," he said, though the dart of his glance over his shoulder suggested otherwise. "The house is dead. The servants are so drunk on nerves and port they can barely see to the cleanup. No one even flinched an eye at my presence."

Alexei didn't move from the door. He pressed his palm flat against the wood, white-knuckled. "You're certain you weren't followed?"

Daniel exhaled hard through his nose. The tap of his fingers against his thigh threatened to set the whole world humming. "I came through the side garden. Circled the maze twice. If the Goldsmids could keep pace, they'd have caught me ten times by now."

Something in Alexei's posture—something I would have missed before a life spent cataloging the secrets of the recently and not-so-recently deceased—slumped. For a moment he was nothing more than a pale boy, ringed by the aftermath of his ancestors' bad decisions. "Then we speak fast," he said.

Daniel picked up a file from the desk and rifled through it, ignoring the way his hands trembled. "You wanted to know who's behind the exhumations in the East End. I have it. But I need you to be honest with me, Alexei. Completely, this time."

East End? Was something like this happening in London?

A wince from the young Vronsky. He let his hand slide from the door, and in a single motion, dropped into the battered office chair behind the desk. The oil lamp guttered and swayed, and I watched the play of nerves across his face —a flash of cheek, a shadow flickering under the eye, the sweat at the hairline already working to undo the starch in his collar. "Ask," he said.

Daniel's gaze was not unkind, but it was merciless. "You

said your family wasn't involved with the Syndicate." He laid a page on the desk, the text side up, as if to defy Alexei to look away. "But this is your father's handwriting. There's a shipment schedule for the next month, cross-referenced with the Goldsmid's ledgers and the Beaumont's port documents in Marseilles. Why wouldn't you tell me the Vronskys have ties to the Syndicate which puts them at odds with Mother Russia? That opens up a whole new bevy of suspects."

The silence ballooned. Sweat darkened the silk at Alexei's throat; he swallowed, and the sound was loud as a gunshot in the hush. "I didn't know he was keeping records," Alexei said at last. His accent, usually sanded to nothing, thickened with each syllable. "I knew there were...arrangements. But I refuse to believe my father had any knowledge of the Goldsmids before I took up with Celeste. They care that she is the daughter of a wealthy Comte, that is all, and the Goldsmids are a proxy and possible business contact they found in Paris." He forced a smile, a Vronsky family specialty, all canines and no warmth.

"That doesn't seem a little too coincidental to you?" Alexei asked skeptically.

Alexei shrugged. "It is an old business full of old families."

"Your father is a Romanov loyalist. He's been funding exiles in London for years. But this"—he jabbed the paper—"this is about something more than a noble marriage. There's a second set of ledgers, Alexei. One in Hebrew, the other in code I haven't cracked. I think your father's trying to play both sides of the ocean. If he's in bed with the Syndicate and with the Emperor, either side will gladly wipe out your entire bloodline."

Alexei looked up, and his eyes found Daniel's. They were the color of rain and disappointment, of cities left behind and women never properly mourned. "I told you. My father does not love the Motherland. He loves only the throne. If the

Tzar falls, he will have no home to return to. And if the Jews of England want to back the Syndicate alongside the Bolsheviks"—here, at last, the mask slipped—"then he will sell them the bones of a thousand enemies for a single seat at the table."

I felt my own mouth go dry. In the lamp's haze, the two men were nearly of an age, but Daniel looked infinitely older. He sat, then, on the near edge of the desk, careful not to disturb the lamp or the neat stacks of death warrants. "Where does this leave you?"

Alexei shrugged, but the movement was an echo, not a statement. "Celeste wishes to marry me. My mother wishes to return to Russia. My father will not allow it and insists we settle in England or France. He fears revolution. But if I am loyal to the Syndicate, I've no choice but to attend to their interest in Paris." He gave a bark of laughter, then wiped his forehead with the back of his hand. The sweat stain grew. "God, I hope to never see another graveyard until they put me in one."

Daniel nodded, letting the silence do the work. After a long moment he said, "You called me here because you feared it was your family, and not the Goldsmids, who incurred the wrath of this grave excavator. You can't expect me to only print half the truth if I find your father is a double agent for not just our enemy, but also our most evasive organized criminal enterprise."

"My father believes the only thing that unites the English is hatred and greed," Alexei said, almost gently. "He'd never have come to England for succor if not for Roth." He gestured, helpless, at the cavern of literal buried secrets. "My father thought the Hammer was a true Russian exile and couldn't escape the Syndicate until the Hammer had already drawn him into their web...Thank God for Celeste. Marriage to her appeases all sides and takes us off to Paris, where both the Tzar and the Syndicate have less influence. And still... My mother will stop weeping for her homeland."

Daniel's next question was a whisper. "And you?"

He let his shoulders fall. "All I want is to live in peace and safety for my family. If my father committed crimes, I cannot stop you from uncovering them."

There was nothing to say, so Alexei filled the air with noise. He leafed through papers, careful to keep them in the order he'd found, selected two and handed them to Hartwell before closing the file with a click that echoed around the little mausoleum of secrets.

"Thank you, Vronsky. You're doing the right thing," Hartwell said, slapping his shoulder. "It's my fervent hope to see you settled with your wife in Paris with a half-dozen little condescending Vronskys gurgling French at you."

Alexei attempted a smile. "The Goldsmids are kind people...but if they suspect you know about this before the article comes out...Not even the Queen could protect you." He moved toward the door but paused before opening it. "The Syndicate's most prolific assassin is in attendance, and he'd slice you from ear to ear and then take Miss Mahoney out for chipped ices without changing his cufflinks."

I froze at the sound of my name.

Daniel nodded, but his face was ashen. He gathered the lamp and turned to follow. "The nebulous circumstances around Miss Mahoney's presence here in proximity to the Syndicate is most peculiar. I always thought she worked in tandem with the Yard."

I did.

I, much like Lord Vronsky, have had to play both sides in order to survive. It's as terrifying a way to live as Alexei—as anyone—might imagine. That the Vronskys, true Russian royalty, suffered the same fate made me feel a little less daft.

"I'll mention Miss Mahoney when I interview the

inspector London sent," Hartwell offered. "This lout is as likely to give me an uppercut as a statement, but Croft knows that information is a good currency. I'll dangle Syndicate information on the edge of my hook and see if he can trade me anything about the political challenges this might cause."

Lout. It was the perfect word for the large, grumpy, square of a man that was Detective Inspector Grayson Croft.

As they passed out of sight, I let my knees go soft and slumped to the cold stone floor, the dust motes settling around me in silent judgment. I listened to the hush that followed their exit, the distant reverberation of their boots, the slow thump of my own heart as it remembered, in the absence of witnesses, to keep going.

I waited, counting my breaths, then crawled from the shadow of the desk lamenting how filthy my skirts must be. Standing, I let one foot nudge a stray splinter of wood out of the way. It broke with a delicate snap, a sound no louder than a dying mouse, but in that tomb-like silence it was a cannonade.

The effect was instantaneous. From the passage outside, the shuffling of boots ceased. Then the door—barely shut— whipped open so fast it rebounded off the wall, sending a fan of dust motes tumbling through the light. Alexei's silhouette reappeared, the lantern held aloft and cocked like a weapon; Daniel was half a pace behind, his right hand deep in his coat, telegraphing the promise of a much less metaphorical gun.

I did what any sensible animal would do: I flattened myself to the floor, rolled behind the desk, and wormed my body into the dead space between the wall and a beam supporting the upper shelves. The fit was so tight that the pressure squeezed the air out of my lungs; my spine dug against stone, my face smushed into the lint-thick corner. If they decided to check behind the desk, I'd be as visible as a painted saint on a chapel ceiling, but it was my only choice.

The lamp's glow swept across the walls, skipping over the desk once, twice, then coming to rest on the nest of folders and bones I'd disturbed moments before. Alexei entered first, eyes narrowed to slits, his breath fast and shallow. He scanned the chamber, then turned the lantern toward the narrow crawlspace where I was wedged, the shadows on my hands turning them into claws.

"I told you there were rats," he whispered.

Daniel followed, his gaze dissecting every square inch of the floor. "That wasn't a rat," he muttered, the words so close I could feel the vibration in the wood beam above my head. "Rats don't snap twigs."

For the next eternal minute, they circled the room. Each of them peaked beneath the desk, exposing my previous hiding place, and I sent a quiet prayer of thanks that I'd not reclaimed it.

I kept my breath slow and shallow, mouth pressed so close to the wall I could taste the mineral sweat of centuries spent in the dark. My left thigh started to throb, then go numb, but I willed myself to ignore it.

Something tickled the back of my hand. I held still, every muscle taut as a deathbed vow, and watched as a spider the size of a sovereign dropped from the beam above, landing feather-light on the soft skin between thumb and wrist. Its legs, delicate and precise, began a slow promenade up the inside of my forearm. My entire body prickled with a terror so clean it bordered on ecstasy.

If I so much as flinched, the men would hear.

Alexei stopped directly in front of the desk, head canted as if listening to the room itself. "You hear that?" he said, voice barely more than a thought.

Daniel, now at the threshold again. "Just water. Old pipes."

"Feels like eyes," he whispered. "Always does, in places like this."

Daniel snorted, but the bravado was all surface. "Let's get out. I hate this hole."

They hesitated for another few seconds—long enough for the spider to complete its pilgrimage to my elbow, then drop, blessedly, onto the floor. The sound of their boots shifted, retreating at last to the corridor beyond.

I waited until the echo faded, then waited again, counting to sixty in two different languages.

Only when I was certain the chamber was empty did I let myself exhale.

It came out in a sob.

I peeled my body off the wall, every joint singing in agony. My hands were shaking so badly I could barely pry the dead spider web from my sleeve. Sweat slicked my scalp and ran down my neck, cold as river water.

The sound of water, Daniel had said. Old pipes.

But I heard it now, clear and pure—the soft, persistent drip of liquid somewhere in the bowels of the house. It was the only noise left.

That, and the shallow, unbelieving laughter that bubbled up from my own throat.

Somehow, I was alive.

I slumped to the floor, legs sprawling, and closed my eyes, letting the darkness wrap me up. For the first time since the night began, I did not want to move. I wanted only to stay in that little nest of bone and ledgers, and breathe, and remember what it was to be merely alive and not yet dead.

But I had too many questions for the dark to answer, and above me the house would soon stir.

I stumbled to my feet, knees giving a brief preview of the arthritis that would one day finish me, and took a last sweep of the desk for anything portable. I took Jorah Roth's folder with me, shoving it down my front between the corset and my bodice.

I surfaced, eventually, into a narrow corridor that connected the estate's lower storage rooms with the main basement. It was here, in this liminal strip of house, that all the disowned artifacts of Goldsmid prosperity were left to rot: old furniture in funereal shrouds, towers of obsolete ledgers, a box of what might have been children's toys but were now just bone and mildew. The air was a humid archive of every bad decision the family had ever made. It felt oddly homey.

I waited another minute, eyes adjusting, heart settling back into its customary place behind my breastbone. Then I checked the hall—left, right, nothing but the faint smear of early dawn leaking in around a storm door at the far end.

I moved.

Not a run, not even a brisk walk—just a purposeful, forward momentum that I hoped would signal to any observing ghosts (or staff) that I belonged here and always had. At the turn into the main passage, I paused to listen again. Above, the house was hushed, its grand clockwork stilled for the hours until the servants began their daily massacre of eggs and linen.

But my mind was anything but quiet. Every echo in the corridor replayed the voices I'd just heard: Alexei's brittle desperation, Daniel's exasperation, the underlying dread that trembled.

If Daniel was right, the stakes were bigger, older, and far more personal. And if I was right, then none of them knew the half of what the Syndicate or the Vronsky clan was really planning.

I turned the corner, checked the main hall—empty, except for the echoes of my own ragged breathing—and began to ascend the servants' stairs, two at a time. My legs, wobbly as new fawns, threatened to mutiny, but I bullied them onward. Above me, the house slept.

At the landing, I paused. This was the crossroads.

Left, and I could make for the sitting room they'd given to Croft to use as an office.

Right, and it was Night Horse's quarters, if he'd even deigned to sleep in them.

I stood there, hand on the banister, and let the calculus of trust run its miserable sum.

Croft was a known quantity. Principled and rigid. He would pursue the truth to its bitter, ruinous end, even if it meant burning the world around it.

Night Horse was a wild card, but he'd saved me more times than I cared to count, and his brand of loyalty, once purchased, was hard to forfeit.

I made the call, pausing when my boots hit the only illumination, a thin line under the door. The urge to knock was nearly overwhelming, but so was the urge to flee the house entirely and take my chances with the early trains to London.

Instead, I waited, ear pressed to the door, listening for any sign he was in. I heard nothing.

I raised my hand.

Paused.

Then, in a whisper not meant for any living ear, I said, "I'd better not regret this."

And I opened the door.

The next move, as always, was mine.

The light in the room was not, as I'd expected, the dying glow of a single lamp. It was the mutual, cold illumination of two men who could not decide if they were adversaries or merely inconveniently on the same side.

Croft was there, hunched in the borrowed armchair, boots planted wide and hands folded over his stomach like a bear at a council of wolves. Night Horse stood by the window, backlit and expressionless, eyes fixed on some point beyond the glass, as if he could see the next murder even before the victim had begun to suspect.

As I entered, the room contracted: two gazes, one weighing, one stripping down to essentials. I realized, too late, that if I'd hoped for a private parlay with either man, I'd just lost my tactical advantage.

Worse, I'd lost my nerve.

Croft looked up first, his face composed but not unscarred. "I see the Goldsmids invite all sorts to their festivals," he grumbled in his Northern brogue.

"Mr. Night Horse," I greeted, not signaling whether or not I was aware of his presence in the home. My voice sounded raw, as if I'd spent the last hour screaming into the underside of a desk. I clutched my skirts, aware that the folder I'd jammed between bodice and corset now felt like a live mouse, squirming with every breath.

Night Horse didn't turn, but I knew he was cataloging my every move.

"Did you find what you were looking for?" asked Croft, and if his tone was cordial, his eyes were as sharp as ever.

"No one finds anything in this house except more questions," I replied, dropping heavily onto the edge of the hearth. My knees still ached from the crawlspace, and my heart had not yet decided if it trusted the company.

"We were just discussing the attack," Croft said. "And the body."

I eyed Night Horse, but he kept his gaze on the window. "I gather you have a plan for the day," I said.

Croft's glacial eyes nearly glowed with triumph. "I apprehended the reverend last night. Blackwood. He's in the village jail, and I intend to put him to the question before anyone else in this parish realizes just how deep this rot runs."

"I'm coming with you," I said, surprising myself with the

vehemence. "You'll need someone to keep him alive long enough for a confession."

Night Horse turned then, meeting my eyes with an intensity that made the room feel smaller still. "You should not go," he said. "He will not speak to you, not the truth."

"He'll speak to Croft even less," I snapped. "Unless your plan is just to break his teeth and hope wisdom falls out."

"Sometimes that works," Night Horse said.

"An effective strategy," Croft grumbled in unison.

The look of surprised disgust the two shared at their agreement would have been comical under other circumstances.

Croft stood, smoothing the front of his coat as if preparing for a parade. "I would welcome your company, Miss Mahoney. But know that the village constable has already been bought and paid for by someone with interests far above this family. If I am to get anything out of Blackwood, it must be done before word gets out that he's alive and in custody."

"Understood," I said. I knew better than to believe in luck, but for a moment I suspected I'd been visited by its dim-witted cousin, timing. "Well, do come along, Night Horse, let the three of us see what the insufferable Reverend Blackwood has to say, shall we?"

"He's not coming," Croft folded strong, stubborn shoulders over his chest. "You're lucky I allow you to trot along."

"He'll just follow in the shadows and extract the information...another way." I rolled my eyes. "Might as well see if his presence as a foreigner doesn't incite the man to incriminate himself."

Croft gave Night Horse the kind of look rarely witnessed outside of dueling grounds or madhouses. "Fine." The lone syllable might as well have been a bullet.

Night Horse, for his own part, absorbed the attention with the stillness of a beast that'd never known a natural predator. The air between them throbbed with equal parts professional disdain and masculine posturing.

Croft said, "You look like you've crawled through a peat bog, Mahoney."

I smoothed my skirt as best I could, trying to crush the file flatter against my ribs. "Nothing a proper wash won't fix. The Goldsmids are a little too fond of their secret passages— it seems their ancestors hoarded not just gold, but mold and seven generations of bad air."

Night Horse's gaze flicked to the lump beneath my corset, then away. If he'd noticed the outline of the file, he gave no sign, but I felt the warning in it anyway.

The silence between the men ballooned, a pressure drop you could measure in mercury.

Croft said, "I hope you can change quickly, we leave in ten minutes."

I slipped into the corridor, let the door fall shut, and exhaled against the wall, my lungs flat as pressed flowers. I crossed to my room, ducked inside, and, after locking the door, yanked the folder out. It was lighter than I remembered —maybe because my arm was shaking so badly I could barely hold it.

For a moment I debated tossing the damned thing into the fireplace. But the pages inside were a map of everything I'd come to suspect: the list of names, the ledgers, the anno-tated letters that made the Goldsmids more than just a family of lubricated merchants and made Jorah's ambitions more than just a disease that could be cut out with a scalpel. I shoved the file under the loose floorboard beside my trunk. Then I raked my hair into something approaching civility, cinched my boots, and swapped my dusty skirt and blouse for the last clean one I had meant to travel in tomorrow.

Croft and Night Horse were already in the vestibule, impatient as dogs denied a scent. I joined them, and together we stepped out into the day: a sky the color of bruised linen, the air raw and alive with the smell of wet grass and the distant promise of manure.

"What is wrong?" I inquired Night Horse when Croft's long stride took him several paces ahead on the lane into town.

Night Horse waited an uncomfortably long time to answer. "I'm wondering why you knocked on Croft's door. It did not seem that you meant to find me there."

There was no use denying it, so I didn't. I watched his mouth twist around the words he wanted to say but wouldn't.

"You think I'm a traitor?" I asked, knowing that was exactly what I was. A traitor to an institution I never meant to join in the first place.

He shrugged. "I know that to people like you and I, survival is more important than loyalty."

That wasn't an answer, but I didn't press him for one.

If he knew what was in those files, he might penetrate me with his blade next time.

Chapter Eighteen

The jail was a parody of itself—a block of mortared misery squatting at the edge of the square, where the dirt road's ambition toward cobblestone ended in the indignity of mud. The fog had decided it wanted to see justice, and seeped into every fissure of the building, beading on the black iron bars and slicking the steps.

"Inspector Croft," the constable announced, and if there was any doubt about who ran this station, the way he pronounced Croft's title dissolved it. "We've kept the prisoner isolated, as per your instructions."

"Good," Croft said, and the word landed like a door slamming shut. "Bring us to him."

The constable nodded, eyes flicking to Night Horse and me. "There's three of you," he said, the arithmetic clearly challenging. "Is that necessary, sir?"

Croft did not bother with an answer. At his look, the constable scrambled to do his bidding.

Inside, the jail was little more than a corridor of cells and a makeshift office. The air had that unique tang of fermenting humanity—sweat, fear, cheap gin, and the slop bucket—and somewhere, a mouse was dying with exquisite theatricality.

Night Horse wrinkled his nose.

The constable led us to the end cell, where Blackwood awaited. The reverend sat atop a splintered bench, hands folded, collar crooked and coat still stained with the evening's drama. His hair, usually lacquered to a missionary shine, drooped in dank commas over his brow. Yet he radiated composure, spine straight, head high. The posture of a man who believed himself wronged by the world, not just the system.

"Reverend," Croft said, voice made of gravel and courtesy. "I trust the night hasn't been too uncomfortable."

Blackwood looked up, his gaze finding me first, then Night Horse, then Croft. His eyes were bloodshot, but they gleamed with the manic light I'd seen in political fanatics and certain species of rats. "Inspector," he replied, with a parody of respect. "You bring quite the entourage."

Night Horse folded himself against the far wall, arms crossed. Croft produced his notebook with a flick, the pencil already sharpened to a lethal point.

"I'll be blunt, Blackwood," Croft said. "There's evidence to suggest you orchestrated not only last night's violence, but also a series of grave desecrations and crimes against the dead stretching from London to this very parish. I advise you to be direct."

Blackwood snorted, the sound more animal than human. "I don't answer to the law of man. Only to God."

I stepped forward, letting the bars chill my gloved hands. "You're an educated man, Reverend. Surely you know that these atrocities—these 'demonstrations'—won't bring about your promised social cleansing. All you're doing is giving the devils you claim to fight more names to add to their ledgers."

He blinked, slowly, as if savoring the taste of my words.

"The Irish, the Jew, and the Heathen," he said, rolling the phrase in his mouth until he spat in Night Horse's direction. "An unholy trinity if there ever was one."

I glanced back to the shadows to see that Night Horse's lips had thinned, but he didn't move.

Croft's pencil scratched methodically. "Tell us about the Sons of Albion. Who funds them?"

Blackwood sat back. "England," he said. "Real England. The blood of it. I serve at their pleasure."

"Who is the man in the red mask?" I pressed, noting the infinitesimal tightening of his jaw. "The one giving orders at your little rally."

His eyes glittered. "Sometimes," he said, voice soft, "one must make a deal with the devil to bring about the Lord's work."

The air in the cell seemed to warp around the words, as if the fog itself recoiled.

Croft leaned in, pen at the ready. "And this devil—does he have a name, Reverend?"

Blackwood smiled, thin as a wire. "You think the devil gives his true name to the likes of you, Inspector? You're a functionary. He answers only to power."

Croft closed his notebook with a snap. "Let me be clear. If you're protecting a higher authority, the consequences for you become significantly more dire. You will be charged as principal in murder and conspiracy to incite violence. Tell me who you're working for and you might live long enough to see another pulpit."

The reverend spread his hands, palms up, the gesture halfway between prayer and resignation. "I work for England," he repeated. "And for England's liberty from the tyranny of the alien, I would die."

Night Horse drifted closer to the bars, all silent menace.

Blackwood's gaze flicked to him and stuck. "You think

you scare me?" he sneered. "Your kind are just the prelude to what's coming. Savage. Unfit. This is the age of the white man. Of steel rather than stone. Of the Nation of God not tribes of pagan whores."

Night Horse said nothing, but the constable, hitherto forgotten, flinched and stepped back. A fragile silence bloomed, then shattered as Blackwood began to laugh—low, guttural, the sound of a man who'd already made peace with hell.

"Ask your questions, Inspector," he said at last, wiping tears from his eyes. "But know this: you're not investigating a crime. You're witnessing the birth of a new nation."

His words hung in the cell, thick and oily. Croft showed a composure of which I hadn't known he was capable. "I want to talk about the grave desecrations," he said, flipping open to a page marked with a red tab. "Six in Whitechapel. Three in Stepney. Three, possibly four, here. In each case, bodies exhumed, sometimes defiled, sometimes only relocated. That's not the work of a mob. It's the work of an organization."

Blackwood's jaw ticked. "I know nothing about that. The Sons are men of faith, not grave robbers."

"You're lying," Croft said, the words thrown like stones. "We have a witness. Said the exhumations started months before the violence. It's logical that the Sons of Albion coordinated both."

Blackwood hesitated, and it was a real hesitation, not the kind manufactured for effect. He started to speak, stopped, then laughed once—a dry, asthmatic sound.

"I told you," he said at last, "sometimes you must make a deal with the devil." His eyes, bloodshot and wild, landed on me. "Or perhaps," he said, "you're familiar with that arrangement."

My gloved hands found the bars again. "We're not talking

about me. We're talking about you, and the poison you pump through your congregation every Sunday."

"Poison?" Blackwood's smile was bitter as quinine. "I preach the old truths, Miss Mahoney. England for the English. Protecting our children from the rot that infests every street. Your kind—your imported morals and mongrel blood—"

"—keeps the world spinning when yours would choke it on tea and dead dreams," I shot back.

He grinned, and the effect was almost charming, if you ignored the decay behind his teeth. "The Syndicate pays you well for that kind of loyalty, I expect."

I leaned forward, so close the bars imprinted the chill into my cheeks. "You think it matters if a man profits by his hatred or by his desperation? You're the same as all of us. You bleed the same."

A flicker of something—real hurt, maybe, or just ego—cracked the reverend's mask. "I serve God," he said. "You serve only yourself."

Croft broke in, voice steely. "Enough. Names. Who leads the Sons? Who was the man behind the red mask?"

Blackwood's tongue worked at the inside of his cheek. "There is no leader. Only England."

Night Horse's boots scraped the stone as he shifted closer to my side, a warning and a comfort. Blackwood noticed, and his next words came slow and precise: "Your bodyguard there —does he know his place, Mahoney? The savage thinks he can protect you, but in the end, he'll only drag you down to hell with him."

Night Horse didn't move, but his jaw flexed so hard I could see the muscle twitch under his skin.

"Tell me about the man in the red mask," Croft said, a last attempt at sense.

Blackwood's gaze drifted to the ceiling, as if hoping for a

miracle to intervene. "He's whoever England needs him to be. A soldier, a martyr, a monster. I never knew his name. He wore the mask so none of us would."

Croft scribbled, head bowed.

I tried again, quieter now. "You can't choose which foreigners are good and which are bad, Reverend. Hatred makes no such distinctions. It always comes for everyone in the end."

Blackwood's reply was a whisper: "You think you're safe because your skin is fair and you're pretty enough to stay the killing hand of a discerning man." He leaned so close to the bars I could see the beads of sweat standing at his hairline, his breath rising in little clouds that stank of bile and clove. "But when we reclaim our island, we'll kick you back to starve with your own."

"We'll see about that," Croft said, shutting the notebook.

As we turned to leave, Blackwood called after us, "Careful, Miss Mahoney. If you lie with savages, don't be surprised when you wake up with your throat cut."

Night Horse stopped, his whole body coiling like a whip, but I touched his sleeve and shook my head, just once.

The moment passed. But not before Croft noticed it.

Outside, the air was warming to the day. Croft walked ahead, lost in the calculus of law and authority, while Night Horse matched my pace, his anger held in check by something sharper than hate.

"Do you think he was telling the truth?" I asked, when we were a safe distance from the jail.

Night Horse shrugged. "He told the truth he believes. That is the only kind of truth that matters in men like him."

I thought of the red mask, and the possibility that Blackwood wasn't orchestrating anything, just riding the wave of someone else's apocalypse.

The village bells began to chime, thin and hungry.

No one spoke until we reached the village square, where the remnants of last night's festivities still hung limp across the façades: soggy bunting, a half-collapsed maypole, streamers twisted into ropes by the mist. A solitary dog nosed at a splatter of dried jam, then looked up, hopeful, as we passed.

I paused to scratch his chin.

The fog was so thick I could barely make out the steeple of St. Mary's, but the bells tolled anyway, as if sounding the hour might frighten back the mist.

Croft stopped at the edge of the square, hands on hips. "That fucking priest is protecting someone and I believed him when he said he'd die before spilling it," he said. The words were softer than I'd expected, the admission drawn out like an ache. "To beat it out of him would have been a waste of time and knuckles."

Night Horse nodded, the movement small but sure.

I tried to imagine what kind of power it took to make a man like Blackwood, a man who'd already burned his own life to the wick, hold his tongue. The thought made me shiver—not from cold, but from the certainty that we were closer to the truth than we were to safety.

We stood there, the three of us, framed by the collapse of a celebration none of us had wanted and the persistence of a winter none of us could escape.

Croft turned, his face pale in the dawn. "I'll start with the shopkeepers. If the Sons of Albion have a backbone, it'll be local. Hartwell's already sniffing around the postmaster and the undertaker—either he'll dig up something useful, or he'll drink himself into a coma before noon." He looked at Night Horse, then at me. "You two stick to the Goldsmid estate. If there's a next move, send for me."

Night Horse pretended Croft hadn't spoken, but I nodded. Croft held my gaze a second longer, as if weighing whether to say anything more. He didn't. Just squared his shoulders and strode off, the fog swallowing him before he'd crossed the square.

I turned to Night Horse. His face was unreadable, the skin stretched tight over his lovely bones.

He waited, then said, "He fights too much with himself."

"He's a good man," I replied, but it sounded limp even to me.

"Good men die quickly," Night Horse said. "Better to be useful."

We set off toward the edge of the square, boots finding their rhythm in the absence of conversation. Overhead, the bunting stirred in the wind, tattered but still flying.

The world was not finished yet.

And neither, I thought, were we.

Chapter Nineteen

The drawing room of the Goldsmid estate had once hosted a prince of Portugal and at least two future bankrupts from Parliament, but at the moment, its most notable occupant was the tea tray, sweating in the late afternoon sun. It glistened on the low table between myself and Celeste Beaumont, who poured with the careful precision of a woman accustomed to handling both boiling liquids and scalding rumor.

The air, filtered through lace curtains and too many generations of moneyed anxiety, pressed against my skin with the density of bad news. I sat on the edge of a settee that cost more than my mother's dowry and tried not to stain the brocade with my own uncertainty. The file stolen from Jorah Roth's underground oubliette—a slim stack of papers bound in old twine and the scent of risk—rested in my room but weighed heavy on my mind.

Celeste watched me over the rim of her cup, her eyes as blue and depthless as a May storm. She was the kind of woman who never merely occupied a room but instead rewrote its gravitational laws. Even here, half a world from

Paris and its daggers-in-the-salon intrigues, she managed to look like someone who'd just set a match to her own past and was now waiting, with polite boredom, for it to catch.

"Cream?" she said, proffering the little silver jug with a gesture so continental it almost felt like a slur.

"None, thank you," I replied, my voice steadier than I'd have wagered.

She smiled, genuine, and set the jug down. "In Paris, the poor take it black. The rich, always with cream."

"An excellent argument for poverty," I said, and she laughed—an octave lower than most women would dare, and twice as sincere.

The file in my mind grew heavier. I'd spent the last hour in a private calculus: hand it to Night Horse and trust him to use it as leverage with the Syndicate, or give it to Croft and watch him prosecute his way through the upper crust of England like an ox in a topiary maze. There was, of course, a third option: keep it, use it as my own insurance policy, and finally accept that self-preservation was more than just a rumor in my bloodline.

I was supposed to be released from Syndicate work once this was over... Should I keep this as insurance against further control?

Celeste poured herself another cup, then reached for the sugar with a languor that belied the sharpness of her next question. "You and Aramis. You are lovers, yes?"

I nearly bit the rim of my own cup. "That's direct, even for you."

She shrugged, delicate shoulders rising and falling like the last breath of a dying swan. "I saw you last night, following him into the dark. And this morning, you have the look of a woman who has either murdered someone or been thoroughly seduced." She paused, stirring with a thin spoon. "Or possibly both."

I set my cup down with care. "Does it bother you?"

"Of course not," she said, and for a moment I believed her. "But I must ask: are you also lovers with Croft?"

The question hung between us, fizzy as tonic in the heat. I considered lying, but her face was the sort that had already heard all the good lies and filed them for future reference.

"We have history," I said, "but not the sort you could sell tickets to."

"Pity," Celeste replied, her eyes crinkling. "The way he looks at you, I think he would pay for the privilege."

My turn to smile, tight and faintly acidic. "He's a man who values his own restraint. I'd hate to see it go to waste."

The truth was, I didn't know what to do with either man. Night Horse haunted my thoughts like a song I couldn't quite place, equal parts threat and solace, a walking invitation to make worse decisions. Croft, on the other hand, was a good detective in a city that ate them for breakfast, and he saw me—had always seen me—for the sum of my bad parts. It was a peculiar comfort to know I wasn't the only one who thought he deserved better than me.

"Do you love either of them?" she asked gently.

I shook my head.

Celeste sipped, then set her cup aside. "If it is not love, then what is it?"

"Necessity," I said, before I could stop myself. "And maybe a little bit of loneliness."

She nodded, absorbing the words like a professional. "Men are dangerous. But you are more so."

I didn't argue. Instead, I let my eyes wander to the far end of the room, where the light caught a decanter of gin and cast a blue shadow across the gold-leaf wallpaper. I thought about the file in my room—the names, the evidence, the secrets capable of burning this estate to the ground—and realized that for the first time since Limerick, I wasn't sure whose side I was on.

"Have you told Alexei?" I asked, changing tack with the desperation of a captain approaching rocks. "About your own history with Night Horse?" I'd never been told by either of them that it existed...but I'm not an idiot. They interacted with the ease of two people who'd been naked together.

Just as he and I did.

She smiled, not fooled in the least. "No, Night Horse was one life-affirming rendezvous after a dangerous deception years ago. Alexei won't bother. He is not so insecure. Besides, I prefer men who are terrified of me, and Night Horse only seems to fear himself."

I raised an eyebrow. "Alexei adores you."

"Exactly," she said, the syllables sharpened by pride or maybe just experience. "I always wanted my husband to love me a little more than I love him. It will keep him faithful."

I made a sound that might have turned into a laugh if I felt good about it doing so. Love and fear. The two most powerful emotions.

For a long moment, we let the silence fill the room, thick as cream and just as hard to swallow. Outside, the grounds men began raking gravel as the efforts to restore the Goldsmid estate were well underway.

I studied Celeste, her profile sharp against the window. "I have something," I said, voice barely above a whisper. "Something that could change...everything." I don't know why I trusted her, but I revealed not what I'd found within the file, but about the file, itself.

Her eyes widened, and for the first time I saw fear, not for herself but for the world she'd built around her. "Does any of the information hurt Alexei?"

"No," I said, too quickly. "Not unless he's inherited his father's taste for betrayal."

She considered that, then leaned in, elbows on knees. "If you trust Night Horse with this thing, he will use it to kill whoever he thinks most dangerous. If you trust Croft, he will build a gallows and hang everyone, even you." She paused, her face unreadable. "If you trust yourself..."

I finished the thought for her. "Then I get to live another day."

She nodded, satisfied. "I like you, Fiona. You're honest, when it matters."

The words stung, but I didn't show it. Instead, I poured myself another cup, the hot water stinging my fingers, and tried not to imagine all the ways this could end. I remembered, then, the taste of Night Horse's mouth—copper and honey, the tang of want and war—and wondered what it meant that I could still feel his hand on my throat.

Celeste watched me with the patience of a cat at the window. "Is it so difficult, to choose?"

"Not the choice," I said. "Just the consequences."

She smiled again, a wisp of sadness in it. "Then you will be fine. Consequences are for people who can't improvise."

We both laughed at that, a brittle sound, and then the world changed in a heartbeat.

The door to the drawing room burst open, nearly unhinging itself, and Daniel Hartwell staggered in, mud-splattered to the knees and hair and eyes wild with urgency. He carried a battered leather satchel under one arm, its flap bulging with the promise of disaster.

"Apologies," he said, eyes scanning the room until they landed on me. "I needed—well, you'll see."

He strode to the table, scattering an errant scone with the force of his arrival, and unrolled a large sheet of paper across the silver and porcelain. It was a map, marked and annotated with a surgeon's brutality: pins in red, lines in black, circles in a sickly, livid blue.

He stabbed at a point near the center. "There's a pattern. The grave robbings. They're not random—someone's tracing a route, one cemetery at a time."

Celeste and I leaned in, our earlier conversation collapsing beneath the weight of this new crisis.

Daniel spread the map like a conjuror unveiling the first step of a trick he'd already solved in his head. The thing was a Frankenstein's monster of parish plans, city directories, and what looked suspiciously like an undertaker's ledger. Blue and black lines stitched across it, some neat, some frantic, the work of a man who'd spent too long in the company of his own ideas and not enough with daylight.

"Start here," he said, planting a stained finger on the Catholic cemetery just south of the old village square. "Look at how the pattern is exactly like the ones from East London. The first three exhumations were all within a hundred yards of this gate. Next, the Anglican yard, just west of the main road. That was a week later—again, new interment, nothing older than a month."

He paused, letting his audience catch up.

Celeste, peering over my shoulder, traced the circle he'd begun to outline. "And then the Jewish burial ground. The one just east of the river bend."

Daniel nodded, gratitude flickering over his features. "Precisely. There's a pattern, but it isn't just geography. It's tempo, sequence, almost ritual." He tapped the map again, this time harder. "They're working in a clockwise circuit. A perfect circle. Always after midnight."

I squinted at the spiral he'd scrawled across the parchment. "That brings them to the next parish over...Littleford, tonight," I said, my finger landing on the cemetery on the map.

Daniel's smile was brief, almost embarrassed. "If we're

lucky, we catch them in the act. If not, we're at least one step ahead for the first time in weeks."

Celeste let out a slow, admiring breath. "You have a gift, Mr. Hartwell."

He looked at her with something like pleasure, but his eyes quickly skittered away. "A knack for patterns," he said blithely. "It's gotten me nothing but trouble, so far."

Celeste rose, smoothing her skirt, and crossed to the bellpull. She yanked it once, sharp and deliberate, and within a minute a footman appeared, so startled by our presence that he nearly dropped the stack of fresh towels he'd been carrying.

"Send for Mr. Croft and Mr. Night Horse," she said, her voice all authority and no accent. "Tell them the drawing room is required, urgently."

The man nodded and vanished, leaving a faint trace of linen starch in his wake.

Daniel busied himself rolling the map to keep his hands from trembling. "If they're using the same route, there's only one real approach. Down the river path, over the old footbridge. There's a blind spot along the north wall, just by the caretaker's hut. They could dig for an hour and never be seen, unless someone knew to look."

The silence that followed was brief, broken by the percussive rhythm of boots in the corridor. Croft entered first, hat already off, coat thrown over one arm. Night Horse followed at a half-pace, his stride measured, his face a mask of indifference, save for the quick sweep he gave the corners of the room, cataloging exits and threats.

"What's this?" Croft said, in lieu of greeting. "You've found something?"

Daniel unrolled the map again, this time with more ceremony. "Not something," he said. "Everything. It's a pattern. If we set up watch here, we can catch the bastard in the act."

Croft leaned over the table, jaw working as he read the ink and scrawls. "Who else knows about this?"

"Just us," Daniel replied.

Night Horse drifted to my side, his eyes grazing the map but never lingering. "You expect violence," he said, voice so low I felt it before I heard it.

Daniel hesitated, then nodded. "If it's the same man as London, he's armed and not afraid to use it. Fast, too—three minutes in and out, even with a body, so he has to bring along some help."

Celeste circled to stand behind Croft, one hand on his shoulder, the other steadying the map. "If there is danger," she said, "you should not go alone."

Croft's mouth twisted, as if debating whether to object on principle or merely out of habit. "I'm not convinced the local constabulary isn't part of the Sons of Albion..." he speculated.

"Just us, then," Night Horse said, his gaze fixed on a spot halfway between Croft and Daniel.

Croft snorted. "You want to make yourself a target, go right ahead. But Miss Mahoney and Miss Beaumont stay here. That's not up for debate."

Night Horse's face barely moved, but I felt the force of his approval.

"I heartily beg your pardon," I said, sharper than intended. "If you think I'm going to sit on my hands while you three bumble through a cemetery in the dead of night, you clearly haven't read my resume."

Croft's expression was glacial. "I know what you're capable of. Which is why you stay here. Let the professionals handle it."

Daniel shot me an apologetic look. "Best we worry about the task at hand rather than keeping you alive, yes?"

Celeste, ever the peacemaker, poured another round of

tea and slid the cup to my side of the table. "Men like to protect," she said softly. "It is their way of showing they care."

I stared at the map, at the spiral of violence and logic, and felt the familiar knot of frustration tie itself around my chest. "Very well."

Daniel folded his arms, shifting from one boot to the other. "We'll meet at the edge of the cemetery just before midnight. If we're right, we'll see him. If not—"

"If not," Croft said, "we get some fresh air and an alibi."

The men rose, each in their own fashion: Croft stiff and impatient, Daniel buzzing with nervous anticipation, Night Horse silent and already half in the graveyard. They left the room as a unit, moving with the gravity of a firing squad.

Celeste lingered, her gaze softening. "You will not stay here," she said, not a question.

I shook my head, the smile that rose unbidden tight as wire. "No. I never do."

She nodded, then left me alone with the map, the cooling tea, and the certainty that tonight would be the worst kind of interesting.

I stared at the spiral, at the slow, inexorable circuit of the dead, and felt my jaw tighten in anticipation.

If the world was ending, at least I'd be there to watch.

Chapter Twenty

❧❧❧

A part of me felt like a naughty schoolgirl sneaking into a cemetery at midnight without a lantern. I'd slept through most of the day, and was at least awake, if not refreshed.

The fog was only knee deep in the churchyard of St. Swithun's, settling into the lopsided graves and sinking, with a lecher's intimacy, into every cranny of the headstones. I crouched behind one of the taller monuments, skirt gathering up the moisture. The moon was three days past full and already cut with the hint of rot, casting shadows so long they seemed to reach for my throat.

If Croft or Night Horse or anyone else had actually thought I'd wait docilely at the Goldsmid estate while they played at intrigue, they hadn't been paying attention these last ten years. I'd never been the kind of girl who let orders go unbroken, especially not when the alternative was gnawing on my own regret in a salon full of bored aristocrats.

A wind picked up, pulling the fog into eddies that made the cemetery seem to breathe. I counted the stones in my sightline—seven, not including the angel that had lost both arms to vandalism and now looked more like a gossiping matron than a celestial host. Each marker was a little drama: the infant, the spinster, the merchant who'd over-leveraged his fortune and died of "cardiac exhaustion," which, in Victorian, meant disappointment.

I checked my watch—three minutes to the hour—then retracted it with a quiet click. I flexed my toes, preparing for the long freeze of waiting.

The side gate creaked. A figure glided through the opening, narrow and upright, moving with the suppressed energy of a man on a mission. Croft. I would have recognized his silhouette anywhere, the way he led with his chin, the coat tailored to widen his already impossible shoulders. Behind him, a shorter shadow lurked: Hartwell, his gait more restless, like a hound on the scent.

Croft stopped three graves short of my position, then turned his head—no, just his eyes, which was far more unnerving—and said, "You can come out, Miss Mahoney."

I debated for a second whether to play at hiding, but the tone left no room for games. I stood, letting the cold sap slide down my calf as the detritus of the graveyard clung to my hem. Hartwell gave a small, surprised start at my emergence.

"Jesus, Mahoney, are you cultivating a taste for haunted gardens?" Hartwell hissed.

"Better than cultivating boredom," I replied. "You're early."

"Not early enough to beat you here," Croft said, his voice dry as old mortar. He eyed my posture, my hands, the bulge under my sleeve that might have been a weapon or just the lump of papers I'd brought. "And you ignored my directive."

"Your directive," I said, "was predicated on the assumption that I obey anyone who isn't paying me."

Hartwell made a small, involuntary noise, the sort that

only came from trying to keep your nerves from leaking out your mouth.

Croft moved in, closing the distance, his eyes gone clinical. "The Syndicate is using you. You're out here on their behalf, and you've not the sense to see how dangerous that is. When this blows up, and it will, you'll be caught in the crossfire."

"You're upset because you care," I shot back, "but you're more upset because I keep showing up the Yard with half the resources and none of the dogma."

Hartwell broke the tension with a soft whistle. "We've got movement," he said, pointing to the far end of the graveyard.

Sure enough, five figures ghosted through the main gate, each carrying a spade or a lantern. Their shadows warped in the fog, giving them an unnatural gait, but up close they were just men—albeit men with more purpose than I'd seen at this hour in a churchyard. They split into two groups: three went for the freshly turned earth of a grave, while two hung back at the perimeter, scanning for threats with a professional wariness.

Croft cursed, low and emphatic. "Five. Christ. I've only irons for three."

"Night Horse would make quick work of two them," Hartwell said, not entirely in jest.

"I left him behind. Can't risk him." But there was doubt in his voice.

The diggers worked fast. The one in the lead—tall, with a pale blue handkerchief tied over his lower face—moved with authority, barking orders in a thick, working-class London accent. They took turns on the spade, trading off every twenty seconds to keep up the pace. In less than two minutes, the coffin lid was visible beneath the churned mud. The lanterns made the scene look almost festive, if you ignored the scent of decay and the undertones of imminent violence.

As they pried the lid, one of the men produced a crowbar from inside his coat, the gesture smooth and practiced. The lid gave with a splintering sound. Even from this distance, I could smell the sharp, chemical tang of the mortician's preservatives.

The man with the handkerchief leaned in, muttered something, then stepped aside for another to reach into the coffin. I strained to see what they were after, but the angle was wrong.

The man in the handkerchief peeled it down, revealing a face made more memorable by the lurid red mask beneath: a domino mask, identical to the ones worn by the Sons of Albion at the Witcombe Green festival. He laughed, then barked an order, and the man who'd reached into the coffin withdrew a bundle wrapped in oilcloth.

"This is bad," I whispered the obvious.

Croft's jaw tightened.

The wind shifted. I shivered, more from anticipation than cold.

"What now?" Hartwell asked.

"We wait," Croft replied. "Let them incriminate themselves as much as possible."

I watched the red-masked man direct his team to re-bury the coffin. He oversaw the work with the detached pride of a foreman, occasionally scanning the yard with a set of eyes that caught the light like a cat's. He was the sort of man who knew he was being watched but didn't care. All I could recognize from beneath his bulky dark coat was his uncommon height, though his stature hinted at lean beneath.

The two sentries at the perimeter had drifted closer now, sharing a cigarette and making a show of scanning the tree line. One of them, stocky and short, held a walking stick that might have doubled as a cudgel. The other looked barely sixteen, but wore a revolver low on his hip, as if daring the universe to challenge his manhood.

As they finished the reburial, the red mask motioned, and the party started toward the side gate—the same one we'd entered through.

Croft tensed, then motioned for Hartwell to move with him.

The diggers reached the gate and hesitated, the red mask sniffing the air. He said something under his breath, and the group fanned out, checking the shadows. It was almost a ballet—the slow, measured sweep of professionals who'd done this before.

It was then, as the men slowed, that a fourth presence materialized at my side.

I nearly screamed, but a strong hand clamped down on my shoulder before the sound left my mouth. I looked up into the ice-bright eyes of Night Horse, his lips set in a line so thin it barely existed.

"How—" I started, but he cut me off with a squeeze.

"Do not move yet," he whispered. "They have someone else in the trees."

I scanned the graveyard perimeter and, sure enough, spotted a faint flicker of movement. A sixth man, or maybe just a ghost of one, moved through the deeper fog by the far gate.

Croft noticed the addition at our side, and for a moment, his expression suggested he'd have preferred an actual ghost. "You disobeyed my order," he hissed.

Night Horse shrugged.

For a second, I thought Croft might punch him, but instead he focused on the grave robbers. "We wait until they reach the gate. Then we flank."

Hartwell nodded. "What about the one in the trees?"

"I'll take care of him," Night Horse said.

I didn't doubt it for a moment.

The group passed within ten yards of our position. The red mask was in the lead, the oilcloth bundle tucked under his arm like a newborn. The others trailed, weapons concealed but easy to reach. As they neared the gate, Night Horse vanished from my side—a blink, a heartbeat, and he was gone.

Croft gave the signal: a jerk of his head, abrupt and final.

We sprang.

Hartwell went high, vaulting over the top of the headstone with more enthusiasm than grace. Croft rounded the grave from the left, a Webley aimed at the red mask's face.

"Police!" he shouted. "Hands where I can see them!"

The diggers froze, but only for a split second. The man with the red mask grinned, then drew a snub-nosed pistol from his waistband and fired, the report sharp and shocking in the cold air.

The bullet took Hartwell's hat clean off, sending it spinning into the mud.

Croft fired back, the round catching one of the diggers in the thigh. He went down, howling and clutching his leg, but the others didn't pause. They scattered, ducking behind monuments and firing wild.

The graveyard erupted into chaos. I dove behind the marble angel, bullets pinging off the wings and turning the stone to chalk dust. Hartwell was yelling something—either a curse or a prayer, I couldn't tell which—and Croft was methodically picking off targets as they broke cover.

Gunfights were never like the penny dreadfuls made out: no one danced or flipped or shrugged off wounds for dramatic effect. There was only the first burst of sound, the blur of movement as bodies scramble for what they hoped was cover, and the endless, glacial seconds of waiting to see who was left breathing when the smoke thinned.

It was a child's grave that saved me. At the first shot, I dropped, face-first, into a plot no longer than my shin, the cross above my head splintered by a bullet meant for my skull. Mud splashed my lips, wet and mineral, but I kept my mouth closed and breathed through my nose—just as I'd been taught by Night Horse, who always said that the difference between living and dying was not how fast you ran but how quietly you lay in the dark, pretending to be already dead.

The world above was a tapestry of gunfire and curses, cut by the high, panicked whine of a man who'd found himself suddenly and irrevocably shot. A body thudded down next to me—Hartwell, by the long-fingered hand that grabbed my arm and jerked me sideways.

"Move!" he barked. There was blood on his face, but his voice was clear, and he was grinning. "Don't be a hero, Mahoney!"

He half-dragged, half-carried me behind a tombstone thick enough to stop a bullet, then pressed himself against the stone and panted, chest heaving. A cut on his cheek that looked both spectacular and shallow.

The shooting stuttered, then resumed, the reports closer together now. I risked a glance around the stone—just in time to see Croft, crouched behind a marble urn, take aim and fire twice. Both shots were precise: the first spun a gunman backward, arms pinwheeling as he fell; the second went wide, but it made the rest duck lower.

I scanned the ground for Night Horse, but saw only the back of his coat, sprawled motionless on the wet earth.

Hartwell must have followed my gaze. "He's not dead," he said, voice pitched low. "Not if I know him."

There was a pause—a lull as both sides took stock. Then the boy with the revolver, the one who looked sixteen, charged, firing blindly as he ran. The first shot took a chunk off the corner of our tombstone; the second ricocheted into the dark.

The others were falling back now, using the monuments as shields, but they weren't running. They were regrouping. The man in the red mask had found his courage, and with it, a plan.

He turned, pointed at Croft, and yelled, "Now!"

Two of the diggers surged forward, one with a shovel raised like a saber, the other with a length of chain. Croft shot the first in the leg, but the second kept coming, closing the distance with terrifying speed. Croft's revolver was out of bullets.

For a moment, I thought Croft was done for. But he dropped his gun, ducked under the chain, and slammed the man in the stomach with a fist so fast I barely saw the movement. The man folded, gagging, and Croft brought his knee up, once, twice, until the man went limp.

The man with the shovel didn't stop. He swung at Croft's head, missed by inches, and overbalanced. Croft caught the shaft, twisted, and drove the handle into the man's throat. The sound he made was small and wet, and he didn't get up.

Hartwell and I inched forward, using the chaos as cover. The wounded boy on the ground tried to grab my ankle, but I stepped over him, careful not to look at his face.

There was still no sign of Night Horse. I scanned the field —nothing.

The red mask was alone now. He turned, bolted for the fence, and almost made it.

Night Horse rose from the earth, a shadow among shadows. He moved without sound, intercepting the red mask halfway to the fence. There was a flash, a glint of moonlight on steel, and the red mask screamed, dropping the oilcloth bundle.

They struggled, bodies locked, each fighting for the

advantage. Night Horse had a knife, the red mask, desperation. For a second, I thought the boy might win—he was fast, and he fought dirty—but Night Horse was faster. He caught the boy's arm, bent it back, and pressed the blade to his throat.

The red mask froze, and every ragged breath came in bursts that fogged the air like smoke from a dying fire.

Hartwell and I charged forward, arriving just as Croft did. Croft's face was smeared with blood and mud, his eyes wide with a desperate relief as he looked at the pair.

"Alive?" he demanded of Night Horse.

Night Horse gave a curt nod. "For now."

Without hesitation, Croft lunged forward, tearing the mask from the slender man's face.

I didn't know who I expected to find, but not in a million years did I think the man behind all this hatred of foreigners would be...

Alexei Vronsky.

Chapter Twenty-One

M y breath tasted like iron as I huffed in the swirling night air.

Croft's silhouette gripped the collar of Alexei Vronsky, whose wrists were shackled with the kind of police irons only manufactured in towns that had already given up on hope. Night Horse loomed just outside the glow of the lantern, motionless and spectral, a silent threat that needed neither weapon nor word.

I watched from a distance of six feet and five years' experience, the cold creeping up my legs with a confidence I could only envy.

Vronsky did not look defeated, though his left eyebrow bled in an admirable arc and his suit was irreparably damaged by the evening's events. He wore the irons like a new set of cufflinks, and his mouth twisted in a parody of a sneer every time Croft's grip tightened.

Croft's face was pure granite. "What I can't understand is why? The Sons of Albion's violence isn't indiscriminate, and your family is at the top of its list."

"Violence is never random," Vronsky said. "Not in this

country, and certainly not under my direction." He shifted in Croft's grasp, then addressed me directly, as if I'd wandered into the scene merely to keep things interesting. "You understand, don't you, Miss Mahoney? You've made a career of cataloging what your betters pretend not to see."

I let the words slide off. Croft didn't flinch, but his grip on Vronsky's collar grew white-knuckled.

"I'm not interested in your philosophy," Croft said. "Tell me about the Sons of Albion. Start with why you desecrate the dead."

Vronsky's eyes glittered with a fanatic's clarity, and for a moment, he looked almost beautiful—if you were the sort of person who found beauty in the twitch before a guillotine's fall. "Desecration?" he repeated, as if the word amused him. He spat a tooth into the mud, then coughed a laugh. "We do not desecrate. We repatriate. The dead belong to their own kind, and I was returning them to the Goldsmids and their ilk with messages they deserved. I did nothing to those bodies that your own Parliament hasn't done a thousand times over, Miss Mahoney. Ask your friend, the inspector. His badge is minted from the bones of ten million Irish and Jews and whatever else you feed to your factories."

Croft's lips pressed together in a thin, bloodless line. "You're giving yourself too much credit, Vronsky. You're no revolutionary. You're nothing but a grave robber."

"You think this is about a few skulls?" Vronsky glared at Croft, then at me, then at the darkness where Night Horse waited, silent as the promise of retribution. "You little Englanders," he said. "You never see the game."

He twisted his shoulders, and Croft nearly lost his grip as Vronsky leaned in, voice raw and wet. "I was made to be a prince. My mother weeps herself to sleep six nights of seven because she cannot hear the language of her birth in the streets. My father is a traitor to the Tsar and to his own blood, but I—" He shook his shackled wrists. "I will not die in this little island, forgotten by history."

He looked up, and his face was a mask of ugly conviction. "The Sons of Albion are nothing. A joke. I needed a crowd, so I built one. If you need an army, you recruit the poor, the religious, and the uneducated. They're always ready to hate."

The words hit colder than the night, but I said nothing, refusing to let his drama find a foothold in my marrow.

Croft shook him once, hard. "Who gives you orders?"

Vronsky's smile was a wound. "What makes you think I take orders from anyone, Inspector?"

"Because you're desperate," I said, stepping closer. "You're not the first man to bury himself in ideology because he can't bear to be ordinary."

Something flickered behind his eyes. Not pain, not yet, but a little brother to it. "I take orders only from my country. My real country." He said it like a prayer, a whisper for a ghost I couldn't see. "For Russia."

Croft let go of Vronsky's collar and stepped back, disgusted. "You're going to spend the rest of your life in a cell, and if you're lucky, you'll die before whatever you've put in motion comes to fruition."

Vronsky laughed again. "Better men than you have tried to keep men like me locked up," he said. "You know why? Because you need us. Your little England would rather have a devil it understands than a saint it can't control."

He shifted his weight, making the chains ring like a wedding bell. "You want to know the truth, Inspector? Here it is: I was supposed to be the Hammer that breaks the Jewish arm of the Syndicate so that Russia may rise. Roth is a relic of the past, a gutter rat who thinks he can rise above his betters. My father—he failed. He bent his knee to the Syndicate. I will not. I will go back to Russia and take my place in the Tsar's palace, and my mother will stop crying herself to sleep, and when England burns itself out, I will be there to feast on the ashes."

"But to send such a heinous message. Why?" I asked.

Vronsky rolled his eyes, the gesture so adolescent I almost laughed. "Because it is easy. Because they are dead. Because their kin will howl, and that's the point of it. The English are obsessed with appearances—you mar their traditions, you mar their whole existence. Jews are especially sensitive to this. Their dead are their anchor, and their customs are their means of survival. To disrupt that is to disrupt what lets them sleep at night."

"You ignorant fuck," Croft drew Vronsky upright, almost nose-to-nose. "And the reverend? Blackwood was your instrument, not your master."

"Of course." Vronsky almost looked offended. "Those religious fools will do whatever you want if they think you hate the same people. I promised Blackwood he'd be a martyr. It's the easiest con in Christendom." He tossed his head, spattering the ground with a line of red. "I even let him think he was in charge, so he'd rally the local peasantry. Beautiful, isn't it?"

Croft frog-marched Vronsky with a thoroughness that bordered on affection. He didn't so much as flinch when Vronsky, emboldened by the lantern light and the faint, tinny echo of distant church bells, began reciting a monologue about the futility of English justice.

"In Moscow, we have a saying," Vronsky said, loud enough for the crows to memorize. "A noble who is arrested before breakfast will dine in his own bed by supper." He grinned, blood drying in spiderwebs at the corner of his mouth. "You can tell your superiors I'll be home by Christmas."

Croft didn't even dignify it with a reply. Night Horse, however, let the silence run out until it was nearly asphyxiating, then stepped up beside Vronsky and said, in a voice that belonged in a very old grave:

"You won't live that long."

The words weren't loud, but they had mass, like the kind of prophecy that caused temples to collapse and rivers to reverse.

Vronsky's smile stuttered. His lips pressed together, then parted as if he wanted to challenge the statement, but the challenge died somewhere between his tongue and the back of his teeth. He glanced at Night Horse, saw something there he hadn't planned for, and decided—sensibly—not to ask for clarification.

Croft glanced at me, just once, the look saying everything he didn't.

Daniel caught up with us at the gate, breathless, hair and coat disordered in a way that suggested both chronic lack of sleep and recent exposure to armed violence.

"They're putting up a fuss at the pub," he said, skipping over the greeting entirely. "Three of the men you winged are demanding to see the village doctor. I told them you'd be happy to escort them to the nearest hospital, provided they didn't mind going via London jail."

Croft grunted, which I thought was approval, and started toward the constabulary with Daniel trailing, notebook already open and pen flickering in the gaslight.

I watched them go and tried to imagine how I'd break the news to Celeste. That her fiancé, so careful and shy at dinner, was now the scandal of the English tabloids and likely to be a byword for at least the next decade. A bigot. A murderer.

A traitor.

Night Horse stood at my side, motionless, the effect amplified by the fact that the world seemed to be in constant motion around him. He didn't speak; he rarely did, when words would only dilute the impact of the night's work.

Night Horse untied the reins to a horse he'd been lent by the Goldsmids, then held them out to me. "You're bleeding," he said.

I looked down. Blood had wicked through the fabric at my knee, a slow bloom the size of a shilling. I'd noticed the pain only in passing, but now that he mentioned it, the limb was beginning to throb with interest.

I took the reins anyway. "It's nothing," I said, and swung up into the saddle with a dignity I hoped would withstand scrutiny.

A breeze picked up, fluttering the hem of my coat and rattling the iron fence behind us. It would rain before dawn, I decided, and maybe—if we were lucky—wash some of the night's memories out of the dirt.

The horse Daniel had left was, to its credit, the only living thing on the lane that didn't flinch when Night Horse mounted behind me. Its nostrils steamed, its shoulders slicked with the evidence of a long, hard night, but it bore our doubled weight without so much as a head-toss. We set off toward the Goldsmid estate at a walk, my knee aching with every jounce, Night Horse's hands steady at my hips.

It should have felt like comfort, but the distance between us was as wide as the avenue of linden trees we passed under.

The world had shrunk to the clip and thud of hooves, the slow, rhythmic groan of leather against leather. It was not unpleasant. It was, in fact, the only sound that seemed honest. We left the village behind—its shuttered windows, its torched bunting still stinking of defeat—and entered the tunnel of fields beyond, where the only witnesses were the hedgerows and the moon, gnawed down to a silver rind.

For the first mile, we didn't speak. I counted my heart-beats, then his. They never quite lined up.

I tried to focus on the night air, the clean sweep of wind over grass, but I kept noticing how he avoided my gaze: the slight tip of his chin when I turned to check the path, the set of his jaw when the horse hesitated at a rut. The arm he'd looped around my waist rested there lightly, as if afraid too much pressure would break something.

I found it infuriating and comforting, in equal measure.

After a while, the horse slowed, picking its way across a particularly muddy stretch. I reached back—an automatic gesture, to steady myself—and my hand collided with his. For a heartbeat, neither of us moved. His fingers were cold, but the grip was gentle. I wondered if it was possible for two people to touch each other without touching the past.

We rode on.

Near the crossroads, where the old Roman milestone poked up from the grass like a fossilized finger, Night Horse pulled on the reins and brought us to a halt. I expected him to slide off, maybe light a cigarette or just disappear into the dark as he was wont to do. Instead, he stayed in the saddle, staring straight ahead.

"I'm going away for a while," he said.

He didn't look at me when he said it, so I fixed my eyes on the milestone instead. The thing was older than the country itself, older than the story we'd spent the last decade weaving.

"Where?" I asked, though I knew he wouldn't answer.

He said nothing.

The moon threw a hard shadow across his face, accentuating the lines and the tiredness that never left his eyes. I remembered, with a sudden sharpness, the first time I'd seen him in Whitechapel—a wild animal in a good suit, daring the city to try to tame him. It had almost worked.

"Will you come back?" I said.

"Maybe."

We sat with that for a while. I wanted to reach for him, say something that would bridge the void, but the words that rose up were all the wrong shape: *Don't leave. I need you. The world will eat me if you go.*

Instead, I said, "Will you find me if you return?"

He pressed his forehead to the back of my shoulder, just for a second. "Always do."

I didn't answer, but I didn't move away, either.

He nudged the horse back into a walk.

The estate was just visible, lights in a line against the darkness. As we approached, I could see the silhouettes of servants scurrying, the gold flicker of candles in the drawing room, the visible machinery of a house returning to its default setting: wealth, safety, denial.

I slid off the horse before we reached the stable. Night Horse dismounted as well but didn't offer to help. He looked at me, and in the slant of his mouth I saw every parting we'd ever had, and every one still to come.

He turned, leading the horse away down the lane, and didn't look back.

I watched him go until he was just another shadow among many.

It was only then, alone in the dark, that I allowed myself to feel the aftershocks: the ache in my knee, the tremor in my hands, the certainty that every good thing in my life was made to vanish as soon as I tried to claim it.

The wind picked up, rustling the linden leaves overhead.

I listened to it and decided it sounded like someone remembering.

I limped toward the house, rehearsing the words I'd use to tell Celeste that the man she loved was now a villain in the history books.

But I kept my eyes on the horizon, where the moon was fading, and told myself that maybe, just maybe, tomorrow would be quieter.

If only for a little while.

Chapter Twenty-Two

T he world resolved itself around me one ache at a
time.

Waking on the morning after a graveyard brawl
was a unique flavor of indignity, and I did not recommend it
even to my enemies. The first signal from my nervous system
was pain—blunt, distributive, and democratic. My wrists
ached from exertion; my left forearm stung with the memory
of a graze that might have come from a bullet or, more likely,
a headstone. My right calf, when I tried to flex it, warned of a
coming reckoning.

The second signal was blood. Not arterial, thank the fates,
but enough to glue my nightshirt to the inside of my elbow. I
pried the sleeve away, wincing at the tacky rip, and inspected
the wound. A scrape only, but fresh enough to bloom a lovely
scab during breakfast. My hands—when had they become so
battered?—were caked with a cocktail of grave dirt and dried
gore. My left thumbnail had snapped off at the quick.

I sat up, every vertebra protesting, and blinked into the
fractured sunlight coming through the lace curtains. The
bedroom, lent to me for the duration of the Goldsmid crisis,

felt suddenly alien. The comfort of the eiderdown, the pretti-
ness of the wallpaper, the painted little birds on the vanity—
all had the air of a doll's house left out in the rain. My blood
and sweat had already left their mark on the white sheets; I
counted the stains with a morbid curiosity, thinking of the
housemaids who would have to answer for them. Some
people haunted places. I preferred to let places haunt me.

It was remarkable, really, how quickly violence left its
signature on the living. The wounds would heal, but for now
they had overwritten all other features. This was the new me:
wreckage-made flesh, holding itself together through sheer
spite and the promise of hot tea.

I levered myself off the bed, found the basin, and began
the work of making myself presentable. There was dignity in
the ritual of it—washing, dabbing, coaxing the swelling down
with cold cloths and the practical pressure of two steady
fingers. I scrubbed my hands with carbolic, watched the filth
swirl away, and wondered how many bodies it would take to
satisfy the world's hunger for drama.

The sound of footsteps on the landing—a hesitation, then
a brisk knock at the door.

"Come in," I said, surprised by how gravelly my own voice
sounded.

The maid entered, tray in hand. She was young, or rather,
the sort of girl who would always be younger than me, no
matter how many years I racked up. Her eyes widened at the
sight of my face, then did a polite circuit of the room,
studiously avoiding the bloodstain at the pillow's edge.

"Tea, Miss," she said, setting the tray down with careful
neutrality. "And a note from Inspector Croft."

She slid the envelope toward me with the tips of her
fingers, as though it might explode. I thanked her and waited
until she'd left before opening it.

Miss Mahoney,

If you are able, I request your presence at your earliest conve-
nience. There are matters to resolve before our departure.

-Croft

It was not a love letter. If anything, the formality of it made me want to throw the teacup across the room, but I didn't have the energy to clean up the mess, so I simply drank the tea and let the bitterness serve as company.

Dressing was a test of both endurance and memory. I selected a sober blouse—dark green, almost black—that would draw the eye away from my face and toward my hands, which were, at least by now, mostly free of blood. I buttoned it with slow precision, each closure a little affirmation that I was still, in some crucial sense, alive. The skirt was navy wool, chosen for its ability to withstand the abuse of travel and sudden flight. I cinched the cuffs, checked my reflection, and declared myself fit for public consumption.

I was, at that moment, the closest thing to professional I had ever been. The bruises were a badge, and the resolve that steadied my hands was pure, uncut adrenaline.

I left the room, every nerve buzzing with the certainty that the world was not done with me yet.

The east corridor of the Goldsmid estate had a peculiar light at this hour, as if the sun were unwilling to commit to illuminating the last night's sins. I found Croft standing in the bay window's wedge, arms crossed, one shoulder braced against the woodwork. He looked out of place, as if the room had been engineered specifically to mock the broad lines of his coat and the permanence of his scowl.

He didn't acknowledge me at first, which was both a power play and an old habit. I allowed myself the luxury of a pause, letting my boots scuff the carpet with the studied nonchalance of someone who'd memorized every possible approach to confrontation.

"Miss Mahoney," he said finally, his reflection in the glass giving him two faces—one real, one spectral, both equally severe.

"Inspector," I replied, resisting the urge to rub at the bruise along my jaw. "You summoned me."

He uncrossed his arms and gestured for me to join him in the alcove. The view was uninspiring: the hedge maze, half in shadow, last night's dew clinging to every surface. He waited until I'd matched his posture, shoulder to the wall, before speaking.

"London is going to want answers," he said, softer than he usually did when we spoke. "You'll be called to testify. The Yard doesn't like mysteries, not when they make the newspapers."

I considered this, then shrugged. "I'll say what needs saying."

He nodded, as if this were a kind of contract.

A silence stretched between us, the sort that would have once ended in violence or something adjacent. Instead, I let it breathe before I said, "I hope Amelia is well..."

His features hardened, as if he remembered he was supposed to be furious with me. "She's only silent for my sake. She holds no ill will against you."

"Will you ever recognize why I didn't tell you—"

"I already recognize," he barked. "I just don't know how to forgive."

I held his gaze a moment longer, then stepped out of the alcove, putting the width of the corridor between us. "I understand."

"Fiona" he growled as I turned away. "You did good work. Even if the cost was steep."

That, from Croft, was as close to encouragement as his pride would permit.

࿔

PACKING HAD ALWAYS STRUCK me as an act of cowardice—an unwillingness to let the world leave its mark on you. But this time, as I stood in the borrowed guest room and surveyed the detritus of the past week, I found comfort in the ritual.

The trunk sat open on the bed, its depths already half-filled with the practical: spare linen, black stockings, the sturdy shoes I'd worn to my first Whitechapel postmortem. I folded each item with clinical precision, smoothing the creases, making the chaos of the past few days submit to the order of fabric and wood.

The bloodstained blouse—yesterday's, maybe the day before—presented a small dilemma. I could burn it in the kitchen stove, but that seemed dramatic. Instead, I wrapped it in brown paper and tied it with a length of ribbon, planning to dispose of it once safely back in London. The paper looked like a child's parcel, innocent and incongruous.

Next, I retrieved the file from its hiding place beneath the floorboard. The weight of it still surprised me. I tucked it beneath a layer of underthings, knowing no customs agent or curious maid would search that deep. The secrets it contained —proof of the Goldsmid family's entanglements, the names of the dead and the debtors—were safer with me than anywhere else. I'd promised myself I'd decide later what to do with them.

A slip of lace caught my eye as I reached for the last items. It was Celeste's handkerchief, a careless gift or maybe a deliberate one, left behind from when I held her as she sobbed her grief over Alexei. The fabric was soft, the embroidery done by hand, the initials stitched in a blue so pale it seemed like a memory. I hesitated, hand poised above it, then tucked it into my jacket pocket.

It was a small thing, but it meant more than I could articulate.

The room, stripped of my possessions, looked foreign—like a stage set waiting for the next act. The bed was made, the washbasin empty, the only sign of my presence the faintest indentation on the cushion where I'd spent the last night. I smoothed it with my palm, erasing myself from the space, and closed the trunk with a satisfying click.

The estate was quiet as I descended the stairs. The staff had retreated to the kitchens or the stables, and the air was thick with the anticipation of departure. I found my way to the entrance hall, where the Goldsmid family awaited: Samuel, rigid in a dark suit that looked more like mourning than celebration; Hannah, her features composed but her eyes sharp as ever; and behind them, a pair of footmen standing sentinel beside my luggage.

The farewell was conducted with all the warmth of a bank transaction.

"Miss Mahoney," Mr. Goldsmid intoned, "we are grateful for your efforts on behalf of our household."

I inclined my head. "It was my pleasure, Mr. Goldsmid. I hope the matter is now resolved."

He offered a handshake—dry, limp, and brief.

Hannah stepped forward, her gloved hand resting lightly on my arm. "If you ever require a reference, you have only to ask."

I smiled, sensing the double edge of the offer. "Thank you, Lady Goldsmid. I'll be sure to do so."

Her gaze lingered, flicking once to the trunk at my feet. For a moment, I wondered if she suspected what I carried. But she said nothing.

The train platform was a half mile from the estate, and

the carriage ride was both too short and eternal. The footmen wheeled my trunk behind me, their conversation muted by the fog. I scanned the lane for Night Horse, Croft, or Hartwell but none were in sight.

Perhaps they were already gone; perhaps they understood that I preferred my exits clean.

At the platform, a dozen travelers huddled under the awning, each shivering in their own private misery. I tipped the porters, claimed my trunk, and found a bench at the far end, away from the other passengers. The air was wet, the mist thick enough to dampen the wool at my cuffs.

The train arrived with the usual bombast, the engine bleeding steam and the windows shining with the promise of escape. I boarded without looking back, found an empty compartment, and stowed my trunk overhead.

For a moment, I simply sat, breathing in the cold and the quiet.

The compartment was blessedly empty, save for a copy of yesterday's Times, folded and forgotten. I ignored it, instead turning to the window as the train shuddered to life.

The countryside blurred, each hedgerow and cow and church spire dissolving into the next. I watched the world recede, the Goldsmid estate shrinking to a dot on the horizon, and felt something inside me loosen.

Packing, after all, was not an act of cowardice. It was a declaration of intent.

I had chosen what to take with me—and what to leave behind.

For the first time in weeks, I felt lighter.

Epilogue

I must have dozed, because the last I remembered was the sun burning through the cloud cover, and the next was the city's outline blooming gray and vast on the horizon. The train's rhythm had shifted, the gentle lull replaced by a more urgent, mechanical rattle as we closed in on London.

A knock at the compartment door startled me from the half-dream.

"Telegram, Miss Mahoney," said the porter, holding out a slip of paper as if it might bite.

I took it, fingers numb despite the warmth of the compartment. The envelope bore my name in careful script, nothing of the frantic hand I'd expected from bad news. I slit it open with a thumbnail and read:

> *WELCOME BACK TO LONDON, FIONA.*
> *I'VE LEFT YOU SOMETHING.*
> *—JACK THE RIPPER*

My hands shook, just a little, the edges of the telegram fluttering as if it could fly away on its own.

I folded it twice, then a third time, and tucked it into my pocket beside Celeste's handkerchief. My breath came faster, the earlier sense of lightness eclipsed by the familiar weight of dread.

I pressed my forehead to the cold glass of the window and watched as the city drew closer, the buildings stacking up against the sky, the factory smoke rising in ragged columns. The train slowed, brakes screeching, and the platform came into view—dozens of faces already turned my way, some waiting for loved ones, others waiting for anything at all.

I checked the telegram one last time, running my thumb over the words.

I'VE LEFT YOU SOMETHING.

Outside, the whistle blew, long and mournful. Steam rose in ghostly veils, obscuring the station until it looked like the set of a particularly bad dream.

I straightened my jacket, squared my shoulders, and gathered my trunk from the rack overhead. The compartment door swung open on its own, and I stepped out, boots hitting the platform with more confidence than I felt.

I was home.

Or as close as I would ever get.

London waited, as it always did—hungry, indifferent, alive with secrets.

Also by Kerrigan Byrne

Highland Stranger

To Seduce a Highlander

THE MACKAY BANSHEES

Highland Darkness

Highland Devil

Highland Destiny

To Desire a Highlander

THE DE MORAY DRUIDS

Highland Warlord

Highland Witch

Highland Warrior

To Wed a Highlander

CONTEMPORARY SUSPENSE

A Righteous Kill

ALSO BY KERRIGAN

How to Love a Duke in Ten Days

All Scot And Bothered

BY KERRIGAN BYRNE AND CYNTHIA ST. AUBIN

TOWNSEND HARBOR

Nevermore Bookstore

Brewbies

Bazaar Girls

Star-Crossed

Sirens

About the Author

Kerrigan Byrne is the USA Today Bestselling and award winning author of several novels in both the romance and mystery genre.

She lives on the Olympic Peninsula in Washington with her two Rottweiler mix rescues and one very clingy cat. When she's not writing and researching, you'll find her on the beach, kayaking, or on land eating, drinking, shopping, and attending live comedy, ballet, or too many movies.

Kerrigan loves to hear from her readers! To contact her or learn more about her books, please visit her site or find her on most social media platforms: www.kerriganbyrne.com